WAGES OF SIN

A James Acton Thriller

By J. Robert Kennedy

James Acton Thrillers

The Protocol
Brass Monkey
Broken Dove
The Templar's Relic
Flags of Sin
The Arab Fall
The Circle of Eight
The Venice Code
Pompeii's Ghosts
Amazon Burning
The Riddle
Blood Relics
Sins of the Titanic
Saint Peter's Soldiers
The Thirteenth Legion
Raging Sun
Wages of Sin

Special Agent Dylan Kane Thrillers

Rogue Operator
Containment Failure
Cold Warriors
Death to America
Black Widow

Delta Force Unleashed Thrillers

Payback
Infidels
The Lazarus Moment
Kill Chain

Detective Shakespeare Mysteries

Depraved Difference
Tick Tock
The Redeemer

Zander Varga, Vampire Detective

The Turned

WAGES OF SIN

A James Acton Thriller

J. ROBERT KENNEDY

CreateSpace

ISBN-10: 1537533193

ISBN-13: 978-1537533193

First Edition

10 9 8 7 6 5 4 3 2 1

For Paris, for Brussels, for Nice and Munich.

And for the next one.

WAGES OF SIN

A James Acton Thriller

"For the wages of sin is death; but the gift of God is eternal life through Jesus Christ our Lord."

Romans 6:23 King James Version

"A friend loveth at all times, and a brother is born for adversity."

Proverbs 17:17 King James Version

PREFACE

According to National Geographic, the Kruger National Park in South Africa is one of the world's greatest nature preserves.

And one of its deadliest.

In the past two years, at least 19 elephants have been killed by poachers for their ivory tusks, and since 2008, over 4600 rhinos for their horns, over 800 this year alone. It is estimated that only 25,000 remain in the wild.

And it is easy to see why poachers are so tempted. At current market prices, ivory is going for almost $700 per pound—and what is stunning about that price is that it is a legal sale, from stockpiles in China.

One can only imagine the black market price.

All to feed the demand by traditional Chinese medicine, and a growing belief in that region that ground Rhinoceros horn powder is an aphrodisiac.

What is perhaps most disturbing is that those sworn to protect these magnificent creatures are sometimes their worst enemies, park rangers falling prey to the allure of easy money, joining the poachers in their vile trade, as witnessed recently with the arrest of two rangers sworn to protect the animals of Kruger National Park.

But what if elephant tusks and rhino horns weren't the only sources of temptation in the park?

What if there was something far more valuable?

How much blood might be spilled for a wealth so vast, it could change a nation's future?

And the knowledge of its past.

En route to Sabi Sabi Bush Lodge
Outside Belfast, South Africa
Present Day

"How much farther?"

"Too far! Another forty minutes at least!"

Archaeology Professor James Acton stared out the back of the customized—and very open—Toyota Land Cruiser Safari Vehicle, and cursed at the sight. Three vehicles, their headlights slicing through the dusk, pursued them, gunfire ringing over their heads as their guide desperately tried to lead them to safety along the dirt road, their vehicle fishtailing far too frequently from the effort.

"Maybe we should just surrender?"

Acton glanced at his wife, Laura Palmer, also a professor of archaeology, crouching down on the floor. Mental images of what might happen to her and the other women flashed before his eyes, and it was horrifying. He shook his head. "We can't risk it, and besides"—he stared back at the vehicles, the distance closing rapidly—"I don't think they're shooting at us."

She rose slightly to see for herself. "What makes you think that?"

"We haven't been hit."

He pulled the rifle from between the seats and checked if it was loaded, the weapon normally reserved for their safari guide, Sipho Tsabalala, to warn off any too curious beasts. It was. He took aim at the lead vehicle, siting the engine block rather than the occupants, and fired. A headlight blew out and the hood flipped up, the vehicle skidding off to the side.

"Good shot!" shouted Sipho from the front seat.

"Lucky shot. Ammo?" Acton frowned as he saw the hood slammed shut in the distance, the vehicle rejoining the chase as ammo was handed forward.

"What the hell do they want?" asked one of the ungrateful brats they had rescued from the side of the road minutes before.

Acton fired again, missing, choosing to ignore the question, their pursuers obviously after one thing—the half-billion in lost gold they might have discovered the location to barely an hour before.

Laura grabbed him by the leg and shook. "I've got Hugh!" She turned away, trying to cover the phone from the noise of the open-air vehicle. He could only catch a word here and there as she relayed their situation to their good friend, Interpol Agent Hugh Reading, their Hail Mary on the satphone.

"Please help us!" shouted one of the young women they had picked up, screaming at the phone. Laura pushed her away as Acton fired, another miss, the vehicle bouncing far too much for him to get off a good shot. They were almost on top of them now, and Acton had a choice to make. Try killing the poachers, and risk their retribution when they were inevitably caught, or continue to try and take out the vehicles.

He decided on the latter.

"Look out!"

The vehicle jerked to the left, throwing Acton clear. He hit the ground hard, spinning with the impact as he tumbled into the tall grass lining the road. The vehicles pursuing them sped past as he came to a stop, the night air filled with the sickening sounds of a vehicle crashing, the screams of his wife, of his friends, mixed in with the nauseating cacophony of a vehicle flipping on its side.

An elephant trumpeted in protest as Acton pushed himself to his knees to see what was happening, the massive beast nonchalantly crossing the road with several others, marking the end of their vehicle's flight to safety.

Laura!

The pursuing vehicles skidded to a halt behind the wreck, their passengers piling out, weapons drawn. Acton leaped to his feet to go on the attack then dropped back down, thinking better of it. He was one against what appeared to be a dozen.

Hopeless.

He crawled deeper into the grass, away from the road, with the realization he was the only hope his beloved wife and the others had.

But only if he stayed alive.

Outside Belfast, South African Republic

May 3rd, 1900

Veldkornet Dirk Voorneveld's chest was tight with fear, a fear he had felt before, and one he hoped to feel again. Yet it was a fear he would never admit to, nor show, the troops under his command needing a strong leader, unafraid of the enemy. On the horizon were dozens of British troops on horseback, and they were but twenty, it thought a small contingent of commandos would draw less attention to their mission.

Though the damned British were having none of it.

After all, they were a small group of Boers and easy pickings.

His Commanding Officer, Kommandant Karl van der Merwe, galloped toward him, coming to a halt at his side, turning his trusted steed to face the enemy. "Veldkornet, take the wagons north. We'll delay them as long as we can. Hide the cargo then return to Pretoria."

"But you'll never survive!"

Van der Merwe stared at him. "But you will."

Voorneveld snapped out a salute, his chest aching with the realization of what was about to happen. His friend and commander returned the salute then readied his Mauser rifle.

"Attack!"

Voorneveld watched helplessly as a dozen of the finest soldiers he had ever had the honor to serve with, charged toward certain defeat, unable to help. He turned to the few that remained. "You heard the Kommandant, let's go!" He flicked the reins and his horse surged forward, turning down the road to the north, the wagon caravan containing the lifeblood of their country fleeing the scene of a battle that would be forgotten in history.

As a dozen brave souls sacrificed themselves.

All to save their nation's gold reserve from the enemy.

Sabi Sabi Game Preserve

Greater Kruger National Park, South Africa

Present day, one day before the attack

"Didn't I tell you this would be great?"

"You did." James Acton smiled at his old friend, Gorman Ncube, a history professor at Rhodes University in Grahamstown, South Africa. He and Laura had been wondering what to do during their summer break besides spending all of it with their students on their dig sites, and decided two weeks away from everything was in order. When Gorman had suggested joining him and his wife for a safari, they had jumped at the opportunity, it one of the items on Acton's bucket list he had never had time to cross off, ironic since he had been hunted by all manner of man and woman over the past few years, yet beasts had pretty much left him alone.

He watched through the binoculars, their guide, Sipho, having wisely brought them to a halt far enough away to not scare the dozens of animals taking advantage of the cool water the lake had to offer. He sighed, completely at peace for the first time in too long.

"Look!" hissed Gorman's wife, Angeline. "Do you see it?"

Acton turned to where she was pointing, Laura rising beside him, both now standing in the rear seat, their heads through the top of the essentially open-air vehicle.

"What are we looking for?" asked Laura, scanning the area.

"See the big tree over there?" They both nodded. "Well, just to the right, in the grass. There's a lioness."

"Oh no!" cried Laura as she spotted it. "She's going to kill one of those poor animals!"

Angeline agreed. "Yes."

"That's terrible!"

Acton patted her leg. "That's the law of the jungle, hon."

"I know, I know," sighed Laura. "That doesn't mean I want to see it, though."

Gorman glanced over at Acton. "Your wife, she's not one of those vegetarians, is she?"

"Vegetarian?" chuckled Acton. "If she is, she's doing it wrong."

"Bloody hell, no!" Laura gave Gorman a quick glance before returning her attention to the hunt. "I love meat as much as the next girl, doesn't mean I want to see my cow torn apart before James slaps it on the grill."

As if sensing she had an audience demanding a show, the lioness pounced, burying its claws into the back of a larger zebra, its teeth sinking into the neck of the struggling beast, its efforts of no use—the most efficient hunter in the world had already won, it now just a matter of time for the magnificent creature it had chosen for its meal, to tire, collapse, then bleed out.

She was patient, the lioness, willing to wait for the inevitable, willing to wait for her prize.

But not everyone was willing.

"Ugh," groaned Laura, turning away and covering her ears, the screams of agony and fear from the poor zebra overwhelming, even at this distance. Acton patted her back gently with one hand, the other eagerly holding the binoculars to his eyes as he watched the vicious efficiency of nature at play. Finally, the creature fell to its knees then onto its side, the lioness tearing out its throat, silencing its screams.

Sipho started the vehicle. "Do you want to get closer?"

"No!"

Acton grinned at his wife. "I guess not." His stomach growled and he patted it. "I'm starving, let's eat."

Laura stared at him in horror. "You can eat after that?"

"Umm, how long have you known me? In another hour I'll be wrestling that lioness for a share of her kill if I'm not fed."

Sipho turned in his seat. "I know a place near here, really good. My cousin makes homemade paap 'n vleis. *Very* good."

Acton looked at his resident expert, Gorman. "What do you think?"

He smiled. "Have you ever had paap 'n vleis?"

Acton shook his head.

"Then you're in for a treat! You never know what you're getting!"

Acton's eyes narrowed as Sipho turned them around, heading back toward the road in the distance. "What do you mean?'

"The meat." Gorman winked slightly. "It depends on what roadkill the cook finds in the morning."

Laura's eyes widened as she turned green. "Umm…"

Everyone roared with laughter at the poor woman's expense. Acton wrapped an arm around her shoulders, squeezing her tight. "He's joshin' ya, hon."

Laura leaned between the seats so Sipho could see her. "He *is* joking, isn't he?"

The driver shrugged. "I learned long ago not to ask what I'm eating." He gave a toothy grin in the rearview mirror as he turned onto the road, Acton suddenly not as hungry.

Maggie Harris Residence

Lake in the Pines Apartments, Fayetteville, North Carolina

Maggie Harris hummed the theme song from Titanic as she washed last night's dishes, a smile on her face, a bounce in her step as she thought of the perfect evening she had enjoyed with her man. He had finally given in and watched the ultimate chick flick—as he had called it—and begrudgingly admitted he did enjoy it, outright laughing when one of the passengers fell down the length of the ship, bouncing off an engine propeller or something. One aghast look with tear-filled eyes had silenced him, and even he seemed subdued with the ending when Jack slipped below the water one last time.

The lovemaking had been slow and sweet last night, just how she liked it. Sometimes she enjoyed the rough and tumble, especially after he came back from deployment and they hadn't seen each other in days or weeks, though sometimes it was nice to just hold each other, stare into the eyes of the person you had chosen to spend the rest of your life with, and enjoy the sensations of two bodies melded as one.

She placed the now clean plate in the dishrack, moving onto a wine glass, hers stained with lipstick, his as if it hadn't been used. A spasm racked her entire body, every muscle tensing for a moment as pain seared through her extremities. The glass fell to the tile floor, shattering, and she gasped out a cry, the pain subsiding quickly.

Barely moments later, Command Sergeant Major Burt "Big Dog" Dawson, the man who had completely satisfied her last night both emotionally and physically, appeared in the kitchen doorway, somehow having made it from the bedroom in what seemed a single bound.

"What's wrong?"

"Wait!" She held out a hand, blocking him from entering. "There's glass everywhere. Get me the broom and dustpan from the hall closet."

Dawson disappeared for a moment, returning with the requested items. He quickly swept a path toward her then took her hand in his, she only now noticing she had been rubbing it, there still pain there. "What happened?"

She shook her head. "Just dropped a glass. Nothing to worry about."

Yet it was a lie. Something had happened, something that wasn't normal, and it wasn't the first thing she had dropped in the past few days, nor was it the first time she had felt the pain, though this was by far the worst.

And like before, her head throbbed with a splitting headache.

Something was wrong, and she had no doubt it was related to the wound she had received in Paris. She had been shot in the head, and there had been brain trauma, though she was fully recovered—or so she had thought. The doctors had said there could be complications, but she had just met with them a few weeks ago and they had said there were no signs of any problems.

Dawson put his hands on her shoulders. "You sure you're okay?"

She didn't trust herself to look in his eyes, instead laying her head on his chest. "Yes. Just clumsy."

He placed a gentle kiss on the top of her head. "Well, it wasn't the wake-up call I was expecting, but I've gotta get ready."

"What's on today's agenda?"

He grinned. "Evaluating new recruits. I'll be gone for a few days."

Maggie peered at him sideways. "Why's that got you so happy?"

His grin expanded. "I get to torture people. Legally."

She chuckled, her pain forgotten. "I'm glad you're on our side."

She turned to sweep the rest of the floor when he wrapped his arms around her from behind.

"I'm on this side." He spun her around, grabbing her ass and pulling her tight against him. "And this side."

She felt his need. "Ooh, is that for me?"

"Who else?"

"Maybe I'll sweep up this glass later. I wouldn't want you going to work distracted."

He lifted her off the floor and she wrapped her legs around his waist as he kissed her with an urgency that told her she was in for a bout of hard sex, not love making.

Her heart fluttered in anticipation as he put her on the counter. "Let's take this to the bedroom."

He smiled. "Is that an order?"

"Absolutely."

"Yes, sir!" He hoisted her over his shoulder, fireman style, and carried her out of the kitchen as she giggled with delight.

It's going to be so *good.*

Outside Belfast, South Africa

Acton leaned back from the picnic table, moaning in pleasure as he wiped his mouth on the back of his hand, his napkin having blown away in the sometimes-gusting breeze. "My God, that was fantastic." He looked at Sipho. "Do I want to know what it was?"

Sipho shrugged. "Probably not."

Laura pushed away her metal plate, daintily sucking her fingers clean. "That *was* good. Impala, wasn't it?"

Sipho's eyes widened in surprise. "Yes, how did you know?"

"This isn't my first time around the Cape."

Acton shoulder-bumped her. "That's my girl!" He turned to Sipho, who they had insisted join them for lunch, they never ones to treat the hired help as hired help. "So, where to now?"

"Back to the lodge. If we leave now, we'll reach there before nightfall, and there're some things to see along the way. You don't want to miss their braai dinner. Tomorrow we'll be out all day, so you'll want to get plenty of rest tonight."

Laura finished her finger cleaning ritual. "Sounds good." She rose, triggering the others, and they all bussed the table to the pleased grin of their chef, a pleasant, slightly rotund man who had tried to feed his cousin's friends for free, something Laura would have none of.

She tugged on his sleeve, pointing to a woman who had a table set up, various crafts on display. "Let's take a look."

They walked over, Laura leading the way. Gorman and his wife took a quick peek then returned to the Toyota, the two proud of their Zulu heritage, Laura shown items on prominent display in their home when arriving two days ago far finer than these local crafts. Laura smiled at the shy young woman manning the table. "These are beautiful."

The woman smiled awkwardly, turning her head slightly and staring at the ground.

Laura held an elaborate scarf up to her neck, showing it to Acton. "What do you think?"

"Very colorful."

"Does that mean it looks good on me?"

Acton went for the safe answer. "Babe, anything looks good on you." His eyebrows bobbed up and down. "Or off you."

She elbowed him. "Save it for tonight."

"Sorry, babe, you heard the man. We need to get our rest. No time to satisfy your primal needs."

Laura folded the scarf back up, tossing him a glance. "Careful, I can be a camel."

Acton's eyes narrowed. "One hump or two?"

Another elbow. "You're incorrigible. I meant—"

"Oh, I know what you meant. Don't make threats you can't keep." He winked. "You know you can't resist me."

Laura gave him a look. "You're mighty confident in your abilities."

"Well, I was there last night, and I like to think I had something to do with what happened."

She gave him a smile, patting him on the cheek. "I'm sure you had some small part to play."

Acton groaned. "Oh, babe, don't ever use the word 'small' when we're talking about that."

She smiled sweetly. "Oh, whatever do you mean?"

He frowned. "Uh-huh, so that's the way it's going to be, huh? Let's just see how you're feeling tonight when you're all randied up and the candy store is closed."

Laura's eyes narrowed. "I thought I was the candy store."

"No, that's the treasure chest."

"I thought these—"

Acton cut her off, raising his voice slightly as he stepped toward the table. He pointed at the scarf. "So, how much for this?"

"Eight rand."

"We'll take it." He gestured toward Laura. "She's going to need something to keep her warm tonight." His eyes narrowed as he noticed a necklace around the woman's neck, a silver dollar sized medallion partially visible under her shirt. He pointed at it. "That's an interesting piece. Did you make it?"

She shook her head, pulling it out so he could see it. "No, my father make. You like? I give you good price!"

Acton felt sorry for her, the woman clearly poor and desperate for money, excited at the sale she had just made. Acton decided to bite. "Sure, how much?"

She removed it from her neck and held it out in her palm, small scars all over her hands and forearms, evidence of a hard, honest life. "Fifteen rand?" she asked, hopefully.

Acton smiled, knowing he was being gouged. He pulled out a bill, handing it over. "Keep the change."

The woman beamed, passing him the necklace. Acton placed it around Laura's neck.

She smiled, holding the medallion then looking up at him. "So now you resort to bribes?"

"Is it working?"

She hugged the scarf. "It could."

Sipho walked over, nodding to the young woman. "Come, we must leave now if we're to make it before nightfall."

Laura turned toward the vendor and smiled. "Thank you so much."

The young woman bowed. "No, thank you. Have a nice trip."

Acton helped Laura into the Toyota, watching as two small children rushed up, hugging the young woman's legs, as excited as she was at the bills she clutched in her hands.

There but for the grace of God, go I…

Swart Farm

Outside Belfast, South African Republic

May 3rd, 1900

"No one can know."

Boet Swart nodded at Veldkornet Voorneveld, his balled fists pressed against his hips. "I'll die before I tell anyone."

And Voorneveld believed him. Swart was a loyal Boer, though not a soldier, instead the sole provider for his wife and three girls. But Voorneveld knew, if push came to shove, this man wouldn't hesitate to die for his beliefs. "You're a good man, Oom."

Swart grunted, refusing the compliment. "I'm a good Christian." He pointed at the hole now being filled in by Voorneveld's men, the gold safely hidden from the rampaging British. "That is *our* gold, not theirs. I'll guard it with my life, like any man here would."

"I have no doubt you will, which is why you have been entrusted with this duty."

"All done, Veldkornet," reported a breathless korporaal.

"Very well. Clean yourselves up and prepare to depart."

"Ja, Veldkornet!"

Swart looked at him and the others. "What will you do now?"

Voorneveld pursed his lips, staring back along the road they had arrived upon a few hours ago. "Join the fight, if there's still a fight to join." He sighed. "I fear the worst." He turned to Swart as his men washed themselves off with pails of water provided by the young Swart women. "If they had been victorious, they would have come this way."

Swart agreed. "Is there any point then? Why not go back to Pretoria?"

Voorneveld shook his head, this man, though brave, clearly never a soldier. "Because they are my comrades, and my friends. If there's any chance they are alive, even just one of them, it is our duty to save them." He swung into his saddle and Swart extended a hand. Voorneveld shook it, the man's grip strong.

"I wish you luck."

"Thank you, Oom."

But I fear we'll need more than that.

1st Special Forces Operational Detachment - Delta HQ

Fort Bragg, North Carolina

A.k.a. "The Unit"

Present Day

Dawson cracked the cap of the bottle of water handed him by his best friend and second-in-command, Master Sergeant Mike "Red" Belme, already taking a swig before the door to the interrogation room closed, silencing the sobs from the other side.

"What do you think?" asked Red, staring through the two-way mirror at the soldier on the other side of the glass, someone who had made the mistake of applying to be a member of the Unit, also known as 1st Special Forces Operational Detachment—Delta, or simply Delta Force to the civilian community. They were America's elite, their existence classified though now well known, their identities closely guarded secrets.

Joining Delta was the dream of any soldier who wanted to see more intense action, who wanted to be trained harder, driven harder, than any other.

It was a privilege.

An honor.

And to prove you were worthy, you had to pass the psychological torture test, for being Delta didn't just mean you were a marksman, an expert at hand-to-hand combat, or a wizard at hacking computer networks, it also meant you were mentally tough, excelling under conditions no average person could fathom.

In the thick of the jungle, or the desolation of the desert, if you were captured and tortured, would you betray your comrades and your country, or would you spit in your captor's face and invite death?

Dawson twisted the cap back in place, regarding the man inside. "He's pretty damned vocal, but he hasn't cracked. If this were real, what with all the tears and begging, they might just believe he knows nothing."

"Do you think it's a tactic?"

Dawson smiled slightly. "Probably, and if it is, he's damned good."

"How much longer are you going to toy with him?"

Dawson shrugged. "Book says three more hours, but I had the clock reset, so he thinks he's only got one more."

Red chuckled. "You're a bastard."

Dawson grinned. "I know."

"How long did you last?"

"Long enough, apparently." Dawson eyed his friend. "You're the bastard who did it to me, you tell me."

Red laughed. "I know. You're the first one that didn't say a word the entire time."

"I think I had a few choice ones for you when it was over."

Red's head bobbed. "Yeah, I can't believe you kiss your mother with that mouth."

"You're one to talk. I watched your video. You're lucky Jethro didn't file charges against you."

Red shrugged. "He shouldn't have got that close. Besides, it was just a nose."

"Yeah, but he never looked the same."

Red laughed. "And the noise it made when he slept. It was like one of those Oscar Mayer Wiener Whistles. I remember the first op we were on together after, I offered to break it again, to see if I could fix it." He sighed, his face turning from fond remembrance to gloom. "He was a good man."

Dawson agreed. "The best. When this is over, let's hoist a few in his honor."

"You bet."

Dawson finally keyed in on something, turning to his friend. "What the hell are you doing here, anyway? Aren't you on medical leave?"

"You've got an op."

Dawson's eyebrows popped. "What, you can't handle it?" he mocked.

Red grinned. "You're on deck, I've got a sprained ankle, and besides, somebody happened to be finishing a debrief when he heard you were being called away and insisted on being your replacement."

"Hey, old man!"

Dawson spun, grinning as two old comrades in arms entered the room. "Jesus, they let anyone in here now."

Fist bumps were exchanged with Rook and Temple, two men he hadn't worked with since the incident in Mecca involving a missing nuke, Rook having left to command his own team, Temple having developed a rare form of macular degeneration that had kept him from the field.

"So you're my relief?"

Rook nodded. "Yup. When I heard what you were up to, I couldn't resist. Not every day you get to psychologically torture new recruits." He jerked a thumb over his shoulder at Temple. "This sad sack was doing the debrief so asked if he could come."

Dawson looked at Temple. "Payback?"

"Damn right. As a matter of fact, weren't you the guy who waterboarded me?"

Dawson grinned. "I did it out of love."

"You were enjoying it."

"Yes, yes I was." He gestured toward the door to the interrogation chamber. "Now it's your turn."

Temple stepped up to the glass, squinting. "Do you think he had any idea that SERE training was the easy part?"

Red chuckled. "I know I thought so."

Temple frowned. "Knowing is one thing, experiencing it is a totally different thing."

Dawson glanced at the broken man inside. "True. But if ISIS or the North Koreans get their hands on him, he'll be in for a lot worse than what he's getting here."

"Yup." Rook slapped his hands together then eagerly rubbed his palms vigorously back and forth. "Can I take over?"

Dawson presented the door with a grand gesture. "Be my guest." Rook reached for the handle, Temple following. Dawson stuck his arm out, blocking him. "Dude, you can't go in there."

Temple stared at him in shock. "Why the hell not?"

"If you can't see the guy, how the hell are you going to torture him?"

Dawson felt something press against his asshole. He glanced over his shoulder and spotted Temple's hand gripping the hilt of an M9 bayonet, the tip ready for a violent prostate exam.

"Found your sweet spot no problem, didn't I?"

Rook and Red roared with laughter, Dawson joining them though only once the knife blade was removed. "Okay, okay, you can play."

Sabi Sabi Bush Lodge

Greater Kruger National Park, South Africa

Acton's thumb rubbed over the medallion around Laura's neck, his arm draped over her shoulders as they both relaxed in a comfortable loveseat, enjoying the idyllic setting, the sun now set, the only illumination from strategically placed candles and fires. Local Zulu dancers were providing the entertainment, rhythmic drumming forcing some who couldn't resist the urge, to jump to their feet and join in.

It was the perfect end to a perfect day.

The sights they had seen had been magnificent, witnessing the breathtaking scene of a lioness on the hunt the definite highlight for all of them, though the viciousness of it still disturbed Laura. Even Angeline had turned away, something he hadn't noticed at the time, her husband later sharing this tidbit to make Laura feel better.

"I've seen it before," was the explanation. "Once is enough."

He suddenly took notice of the sensations transmitted to his relaxed subconscious, and his thumb froze. "Can I see the medallion?"

Laura leaned forward and removed it from around her neck, handing it to him. "Why?"

He ran his thumb over the front, the image of a lioness head not of interest, though it was what had attracted him to the medallion in the first place, the perfect representation of the woman he loved, and a nice little souvenir of their time here. He didn't expect her to wear it when they returned home, the trinket merely a curiosity that would occupy a small space in their shared office already filled with items collected over decades of two distinguished careers. Pulling a candle closer to him, he flipped the medallion over, revealing the back. His eyes widened slightly as the candlelight revealed what his thumb had suggested.

It was engraved.

But the light was too dim to make out what was written. He pulled his phone from his pocket and turned on the flashlight feature, apologizing to those around him, it nearly blinding. He quickly turned it off, though not before he got enough of a look to send a rush of adrenaline through his system.

Could it be?

Anantachin Buddhist Monastery
Cameron, North Carolina

Sergeant Carl "Niner" Sung gave one final bow then rose, his prayer for the dead finished. It had been his first chance to properly honor the woman who he had barely known, yet had such an impact on him—Yunhui Kim. He still found himself dwelling on the fantasy of what could have been, rather than the reality of what was—a few hours together under harrowing circumstances, ending with the promise of a home-cooked meal and perhaps something more.

Though that hadn't been the end.

The end had been a bullet to the head, a bullet that if she hadn't been talking to him, if she had instead kept her head down like the others, would have completely missed her, leaving her alive today.

He sighed, closing his eyes once more, picturing her beautiful face, the image quickly replaced by the horror of the side of her head, matted in blood, unmoving, the smile that had won him over, gone.

It wasn't his fault. He knew that. The bastard operating the drones was to blame, and he refused to ruin his life because of something that wasn't his responsibility.

She was gone.

And there was nothing he could do about it beyond what he had already done—put a bullet in the asshole's head.

He bowed slightly, clasping his hands in front of him as he closed his eyes one last time.

Goodbye, Yunhui.

He sucked in a deep breath then headed outside, his best friend, Sergeant Jerry "Jimmy Olsen" Hudson sitting on the hood of his black Charger, waiting patiently.

"All set?"

Niner nodded. "Yup."

Jimmy waved his phone. "Good. We've got an op."

Niner smiled weakly. "Perfect. I need something to keep my mind off things."

Colonel Clancy's Office, The Unit
Fort Bragg, North Carolina

"Go home, Maggie."

Maggie Harris looked up from her monitor, so engrossed in her work she hadn't noticed her boss and her fiancé's Commanding Officer, Colonel Thomas Clancy, standing at the outer door of the office. She smiled. "I will, I just need a few minutes or your schedule for Monday is going to be a mess and you won't know what to do with yourself."

Clancy chuckled. "What would I do without you?"

Maggie shrugged. "I don't know, but you'd be lost."

"I have no doubt." He rested his briefcase on the corner of her desk. "Did BD get a chance to say goodbye to you?"

She nodded, the love of her life deployed unexpectedly, though the unexpected in his business was to be expected, and with her working for his CO, she counted herself lucky she was privy to what he did for a living, unlike most fiancées. "We got about sixty seconds. Better than most."

Clancy lifted his briefcase, an understanding smile on his face. "Try not to worry too much this weekend." He was a great boss, and Dawson and the other members of Bravo Team respected him tremendously. He understood and adhered to the concept of no man left behind, and backed his men all the way, even if their government wouldn't. He was a soldier's soldier, and according to Dawson, the best CO he had ever worked with.

She shrugged. "I make no promises." She leaned back in her chair. "Plans this weekend?"

"Sister-in-law is in town, so I'm going fishing."

"Sounds like fun."

"It does. Unfortunately, my wife will probably nix my plans."

"I could always have you paged."

Clancy grinned. "If you receive a 9-1-1 from me, you'll know why." He opened the door. "Enjoy your weekend, and try not to worry."

She smiled. "You too. And again, no promises."

Clancy stepped into the hall, closing the secure door behind him, the electronic lock clicking, sealing her inside. She quickly fired off several meeting request responses, juggling the man's busy schedule, when a pain raced up her arm, her head pounding as if it were about to explode. She gasped in pain, unable to cry out as she slipped to the floor.

And out of sight.

Sabi Sabi Bush Lodge

Greater Kruger National Park, South Africa

"Good thing you travel with that."

Acton glanced briefly at the satchel that followed him around the world, containing all the tools any self-respecting archaeologist wouldn't be caught dead without. At the moment, he was taking a rubbing of the back of the medallion in their hotel room, everyone eagerly anticipating the end result, not yet filled in on his suspicions. He winked at his friend. "Don't tell me you don't take your kit with you."

Gorman leaned back, a brief look of shame spreading across his face. "I'm afraid my days of crawling around dig sites are over with." He slapped his belly. "This would be constantly getting in the way."

Acton grinned at him. "A few weeks on a dig and you might just leave that behind."

Gorman chuckled. "This is true, this is true, but I'm too old for that now. Now, I teach the youngsters who will replace us."

"A worthy task." Acton lay the rubbing wax aside, holding up his handiwork. He pulled his magnifying glass from its holder and examined the writing. And smiled. "I knew it!"

Gorman leaned forward. "What?"

Acton handed the rubbing to him along with the magnifying glass. "Is that what I think it is?"

Gorman peered through the lens, his eyes widening with each passing moment. "It couldn't be." He shook his head. "It can't be."

"No?" Acton gestured toward it. "Turn it around and hold it up to the light."

Gorman complied, shaking his head, the reversed letters now obvious to everyone. Laura grabbed the laptop and attacked the keyboard, their satphone acting as an extremely expensive hotspot. She spun it around so her husband could see, an image from the Smithsonian site displayed.

Acton smiled.

He pushed the laptop toward Gorman. "You tell me if what you're holding isn't an exact match to that."

Gorman's jaw dropped as he leaned toward the laptop, holding the rubbing up beside the screen. Laura held the medallion on the other side. "But it can't be! This has been lost for over a century!"

Outside Colonel Clancy's Office, The Unit

Fort Bragg, North Carolina

Jeb stood back while the security guard swiped his pass, the panel to the right of the door switching from red to green. Security was tight, whatever went on here ultra-top secret, or whatever, it far above his pay grade as a janitor. The company he worked for was contracted to push mops and vacuum cleaners, empty out garbage cans, and clean up messes should they occur.

His job was easy, if menial.

He had worked in all manner of buildings staffed by all manner of people over the past ten years, and these military types were the cleanest—or at least the neatest. The worst were high school locker rooms—the girls especially. He didn't know what the hell they were doing in there, but it was nasty. This job was a dream compared to that one.

The guard stepped back, moving down the hallway to radio in an update, their conversation non-existent, this one taking his job entirely too seriously, which suited Jeb just fine, especially today. His earbuds were planted firmly where they should be, Michael Bublé blaring.

I've got to learn to like this shit if I ever want to score with Tracy.

It was growing on him, it not that difficult, already a begrudging fan of the holographic crooner Vic Fontaine on Deep Space Nine. And whenever he heard a classic like Fly Me To The Moon, he found his toe tapping, so it shouldn't have been a surprise that Bublé would have somc appcal.

But two hours at a concert, hearing nothing but?

Ugh, why did you have to tell her you loved Bublé?

He went to flick the lights on when he realized they already were.

Somebody was in a hurry.

He pushed the vacuum cleaner around the front of the outer office, the inner office, where the bigwig worked, off limits. He could feel through his hand that nothing was being sucked up, this office always nearly immaculate. He swore whoever worked the desk vacuumed herself.

Next damned time you start dating a woman, always tell her the truth, rather than what you think *she wants to hear.*

He reached around, shoving the vacuum cleaner on either side of the desk, not bothering with behind, it a waste of time.

She doesn't care if you love Bublé, she doesn't expect you to. She only cares that you won't tease her for liking him.

And it made sense. What guy actually likes Bublé? The legends like Sinatra, sure, but Bublé?

She just wants you to be her plus one.

And that he was willing to do. It would be their third date. And that meant sexy-times when it was over. Two hours of some Canadian crooner was worth a night with Tracy.

Just don't make her think it's a chore for you to be there, and you're in.

A smile crept up one side of his face.

Literally!

He backed out of the office when his eyes narrowed.

Huh. That's odd.

The receptionist's—or whatever they called them today—monitor was still on, though in power saving mode, something he had never noticed before. His eyebrows rose. And her cellphone sat on her desk, in plain view.

Must have left in a real *hurry.*

He paused for a moment, wondering if he should mention it to the guard, then decided against it. He had seen her before, and she was smokin' hot, and he didn't want to get her in trouble. He glanced over his shoulder then stepped back inside, pressing the power button for the monitor, then placing a file that sat to the side overtop the phone in case someone less honest than him should happen to come through here over the weekend.

He flicked off the lights and stepped into the hall, starting to pull the door closed behind him.

He paused.

What was that? A moan?

He removed one of the earbuds and listened, hearing nothing except Bublé in the other ear. He shrugged, shutting the door.

Must be hearing things.

He pushed the earbud back in and moved on to the next office, his escort swiping his pass on the next pad, Jeb picturing Tracy in the back seat of his car.

Bublé, buddy, you better put her in the mood.

Sabi Sabi Bush Lodge

Greater Kruger National Park, South Africa

Acton tossed one final time, spotting a sliver of light breaking around the edges of the blackout curtains in their room. Leaping out of bed, he rushed to the window and poked his head between the fabric to make sure.

Sunrise!

Laura groaned. "What time is it?"

Acton checked his watch. "You don't want to know."

Laura pushed up on her elbows, staring at him. "I haven't seen you this excited since we found Cleopatra's tomb."

Acton turned toward her. "Yeah, and look how that turned out."

Laura gave him a look, holding out her hand. "I hardly think terrorists are going to swoop in and try to destroy our find this time."

Acton took her hand, shaking it. "Hi, Jim Acton, bad luck magnet. Pleased to meet you."

Laura yanked his hand, hauling him into the bed with her then flipped him over, mounting him. "How about one last romp before whatever horrible thing you think is going to befall us, arrives?"

Acton grinned as she lifted the t-shirt she wore over her head, revealing her assets. "Now *that's* a treasure chest."

She dropped on top of him, her lips slowly covering every inch of his neck and chest, half-mast not lasting long. "Ooh, somebody's ready pretty quick."

Acton groaned. "Babe, small and quick, small and quick. Two words to avoid."

Laura reached down and squeezed. "Nothing small down here."

Acton groaned for an entirely different reason. "That's better."

His phone vibrated on the nightstand, a text message arriving. Maintaining a firm grip, Laura leaned over and read it. "It's Gorman, he wants to know if we're ready."

"Tell him ten minutes."

Laura eyed him. "Hey, I thought 'quick' was a four letter word."

"Twenty?"

Laura smiled. "That's better."

Outside Belfast, South African Republic

May 3rd, 1900

Veldkornet Voorneveld brought his horse to a halt, the horror in front of him unspeakable. Bodies were strewn about, several of the horses dead or dying, the crossroads tinged with a red that hadn't been there before. He turned to his korporaal.

"Korporaal, check for survivors."

"Ja, Veldkornet." The man's voice was subdued, nobody talking, an eerie calm surrounding the entire area, as if even Mother Nature knew not to disturb the newly departed. He urged his horse forward slightly as he surveyed the horizon, making certain the British rooineks were nowhere near, about to spring a trap on them.

He saw nothing.

These men were the best of the best. Commandos. The idea had been to send a large diversionary force to the west, their smaller force to the north, the hope they wouldn't draw any attention clearly a mistake.

But the gold was safe, their mission a success, though at what price?

"Veldkornet!"

He spun in his saddle and saw his korporaal kneeling beside a body, a body he cradled in his arms. Voorneveld leaped from his horse and sprinted toward who he now recognized as his commanding officer—his friend. "Karl!"

His korporaal gently lay him back on the grass as Voorneveld knelt by his friend's side, wiping the hair from his eyes. "Are you okay?" But he already knew the answer. Dark blood oozed from his stomach and he was paler than any man he had ever seen. His eyes fluttered open.

"I ordered you to Pretoria."

"Court martial me when we get there."

Van der Merwe laughed then winced. "The gold?"

"Buried where no one will find it, on Boet Swart's farm."

Van der Merwe nodded slightly. "A-a good man. He won't talk."

"Veldkornet! British!"

Voorneveld spun toward his korporaal who pointed to the east. Voorneveld cursed, staring down at his commander. "They must have known, how else could they have been waiting for us?"

Van der Merwe reached up and grabbed him by the collar. "They can't take anyone alive. If they do, they'll torture you until you talk."

Voorneveld took his friend's hand. "I understand."

Van der Merwe let him go. "Now, give me a weapon, in case it's needed."

Voorneveld hesitated, knowing what his friend truly meant.

"That's an order, Veldkornet."

Voorneveld nodded, closing his eyes for a moment as his men took cover, opening fire on the advancing enemy. He pulled his sidearm and pressed it into his friend's hand. "Goodbye, my friend."

Van der Merwe winced out a nod, his head falling back onto the grass, his chest heaving its final breaths as he squeezed his eyes shut.

Voorneveld grabbed the reins of his horse. "Fall back to the south, away from the farm. Not a man here must be taken, understood?"

"Ja, Veldkornet!"

Voorneveld raised his fist in the air. "For the Republic!"

His men roared in response, falling back along the road, using their horses as shields, knowing the moment they mounted for an escape, they'd be picked off. Voorneveld took aim and fired, downing one of the bold bastards as the enemy marched toward them in the open. His men continued to return fire, deliberately picking their targets, commandos far better shots than the frontline British, but there were simply too many.

This battle would be lost.

Though not the war.

Not the country.

The gold was safe, and when they were victorious, it would be returned to Pretoria.

Voorneveld gasped as he fired, sending the shot harmlessly into the ground yards ahead of its intended target, a sudden thought occurring to him.

If we all die here today, then only the farmer knows where the gold is.

He turned to the korporaal. "You need to get back to Pretoria, tell them where the gold is. We'll cover you."

"Ja, Veldkornet!" He jumped on the back of his horse, crouched as low as possible as he urged his steed forward. As it gained speed, a bullet tore into its hindquarters and it reared up, whinnying in agony before tumbling onto its side, crushing the young rider beneath him. Two of his men rushed to help, one cut down within a few steps, the other reaching the struggling rider, only to be shot in the shoulder.

Voorneveld looked about as his men died around him, realizing his folly, and why he should have obeyed his friend's orders.

No one will know where the gold is!

A single shot from a Mauser C96 semi-automatic pistol, its sound distinct, rang out behind him. He glanced back and saw the weapon gripped in his friend's hand lying next to his head, the ultimate sin committed, condemning himself to an eternity of damnation to save the future of the country he loved.

You can't die here today!

Sabi Sabi Bush Lodge

Greater Kruger National Park, South Africa

Present Day

"I highly recommend you take one of our vehicles."

Acton turned toward the conversation, the clear sound of desperate pleading piquing his interest. Four young tourists were standing near a Jag SUV, one of the hotel staff wagging his finger at a defiant young woman demanding to know why.

"To go in this on your own is too dangerous."

She stared at the heap the guide pointed at. "You expect us to drive in that? Do you realize back home I drive a Bentley? Do you realize how hard it was to find this rental in Pretoria? Do you realize how much I'm paying to rent this damned thing?"

The staff member kept his composure despite the derision in the young woman's voice. "I'm sure it is very expensive, miss, but it is not reliable. You cannot go out into the reserve in a vehicle that could break down."

"What do you mean it's not reliable? It's a Jag!"

"Exactly!" The exasperation in the man's voice was comical, as if he couldn't believe she didn't understand the reason for his concern.

Laura chuckled, exchanging a knowing smile with Acton. "I'd listen to him if I were her," she muttered as they walked by.

One of the young men with the Jag lover spun toward them. "What did you say?"

Laura glanced at him. "I was speaking to my husband."

He jabbed a finger at her. "Mind your own business, bitch!"

Acton stopped and turned toward the young man. "Now there's no need for language like that."

The kid stepped forward, the other young man in the group, it evidently two couples, stepping up behind him. "Oh, tough guy, huh? What are you going to do about it, old man?"

Acton smiled slightly. "Let you live to tell your friends what great advice I gave you." He turned to continue with the others when the punk reached out and grabbed Acton by the shoulder, spinning him around. Acton looked at the hand, then the kid.

"Three seconds."

"Three seconds then what?"

"Time's up." Acton grabbed the hand, lifting it high and bending the wrist under as he stepped forward. The mouth cried out as he dropped to his knees, grasping at the hyperflexed wrist in agony, his backup not sure what to do, taking hesitant steps forward to help, then back. Acton bent over and whispered in the young man's ear. "Now, are we done here?"

"Y-yes."

"Good." Acton let go of the hand and the young man collapsed to the ground, cradling it in his other arm. Acton pointed at the Jag, looking at the girl. "Listen to your guide. He knows what he's talking about." Acton turned to leave, giving one last glance over his shoulder at the fuming girl, who left it to the other two to help the moron to his feet. "And if he's your boyfriend, find a better one. His mouth could get you in trouble one day."

Acton helped Laura into their expert approved safari vehicle, then climbed in after her, no one saying anything, though their guide, Sipho, had a huge grin as he put the vehicle in gear, pulling away. Laura broke the silence as soon as they were out of earshot.

"I can't believe kids today. No respect for their elders!"

Acton gave her a look. "Who are you calling elder?"

"Well, I'm the young one in this relationship."

"Yeah, but I'm the hero. Did you see what I did for you back there? I defended your honor!"

Laura took his chin in her hand, wiggling it back and forth like she would a baby's. "Yes, you did do that. Thank you." She gave him a peck on his squished lips then winked. "Old man."

Colonel Clancy's Office, The Unit
Fort Bragg, North Carolina

Maggie groaned, her eyes fluttering open as her head throbbed. She looked about as she oriented herself, then gasped, everything flooding back.

I'm still in the office!

She pushed herself to her knees, resting her elbows on the desk, then with what shouldn't have been a herculean effort, forced herself into her chair. She leaned back, catching her breath, before finally taking in her surroundings. The lights were out, which was odd. It meant someone had to have been in here.

Then why didn't they help me?

She glanced at where she had been lying and realized no one would have seen her if they didn't round the desk.

I need to get out of here.

She reached for her cellphone, it not there, the files on her desk moved.

What happened here?

She moved the out of place file and found her phone. She pushed the button, nothing happening. She pressed again, and again nothing.

The battery's dead? How long was I out?

She checked the clock on the wall and gasped.

Eight hours!

She reached for the desk phone to call for help when she felt another wave of pain sweep over her right side, her head hammering as she slid from the chair once again.

What's happening to me?

Outside Belfast, South Africa

Laura frowned as the Jag blasted past them on the dirt road, a middle-finger salute waving out the passenger side window. She glanced at her husband. "I think you made a friend."

He smiled. "His parents must be so proud."

"Can you imagine doing something like that when you were his age?"

"Nope. My father would have kicked my ass if he heard I called a woman a bitch then tried to provoke a fight."

Laura smiled. "Having met him, I believe he would have."

Sipho glanced over his shoulder. "We're here."

He pulled in beside the Jag, Laura again frowning as she spotted the two girls at the souvenir stand, Little Miss Priss pushing around the merchandise as if it were worthless, the other girl, to her credit, appearing slightly embarrassed.

"This stuff is junk. You actually charge people money for this?"

The young South African woman said nothing, her eyes welling with tears, her lips trembling.

"I think she's going to cry!" laughed the asshole whom apparently hadn't learned his lesson.

"I've had enough of this," muttered James, stepping toward the scene when Laura extended an arm, blocking him.

"Allow me." She walked over to the table, inserting herself between the two girls. She smiled sweetly at the young South African. "Hi there, remember me?"

The young woman nodded, wiping her eyes dry.

"I just had to come back and buy some more of your beautiful scarves. I've never seen anything like them back home."

"Probably shops at Walmart," tittered the spoiled brat.

Laura smiled at her. "Honey, money can buy a lot of things, but it clearly can't buy class." The girl's jaw dropped. "Now, why don't you and your friends move along while the grownups do business? I'm sure your daddy's trust fund can be spent elsewhere."

"Hey! You can't talk to my girlfriend like that!"

Laura turned to the moron who still hadn't figured out how to control the big hole in his face. "Oh, sweetie, you have no idea how close you are to having your ass kicked by a woman." She flicked her wrist. "Now go, I'm done with you." She turned her back on them, running her hand along the scarves. "I'll take all of them." She handed over several bills as the four brats milled about, unsure of what to do. The woman's tear filled eyes beamed as she took the bills, Laura waving off any change.

She took the scarves and turned to hand them to James when the boyfriend jammed a finger in her face. Before he could say anything, she grabbed the finger, twisting hard, once again sending the young man to his knees. "That's the second time you've been on your knees today." She bent over and whispered in his ear, loud enough for his friends to hear, "You seem to like this position. Who's the bitch now?" She pushed him away and handed the scarves to her husband, then turned back to the young vendor. "My husband and I would like to buy you lunch, and discuss this." She tapped the medallion around her neck.

The young woman grinned now, her tears forgotten. "I-I would like that."

The boyfriend climbed to his feet, stumbling away. "Come on, let's go. That bitch is crazy!"

James walked quickly toward him. "Don't be using that word around me!"

The mouth scurried away and four doors quickly slammed shut in the Jag, it peeling away in a cloud of dust. James walked over with the Ncubes. "That looked like fun."

"It was!" Laura patted her chest, her heart racing. "Nothing like a confrontation with the upper crust of society to get the heart pumping."

They led the young woman to a nearby picnic table, orders placed for a repeat of yesterday's meal, introductions made, the young woman Florence Mokoena.

Laura removed the medallion, placing it on the table. "What can you tell me about this?" She flipped it over, showing the impression on the back.

Florence shrugged. "I don't know. I—" Her head dropped, shame washing over her face as tears welled once again. "I-I can't read."

Laura reached out and took her hand, squeezing it. "That's nothing to be ashamed of. It's not your fault." She bent down further, peering up into the young woman's eyes. "And believe me, there's plenty of people back in America and Britain who can't read either."

Florence looked up slightly, her eyes wide. "Really?"

Laura nodded. "Absolutely." She patted her hand. "Sweetie, never, ever, think you're stupid just because you can't read. You never had a chance to learn. I'm sure if you did, you'd be a wizard at it."

Florence beamed. "Like Harry Potter?"

Laura laughed. "Exactly." She cocked her head slightly to the side. "How do you know about Harry Potter?"

"I saw a movie with him." She lowered her head. "I like Hermione."

Laura lowered her voice, leaning in. "She's my favorite too!"

Florence smiled at Laura, apparently pleased they had something in common. She pointed at the medallion. "What you like to know?"

"Just where you got it."

"My father make."

Laura felt goosebumps rush over her body. "How?"

Florence shrugged. "I don't know. He make when he have time, if Mr. Erasmus lets him."

"Who is Mr. Erasmus?"

"He own farm my father work at."

"Can we meet your father?"

She nodded. "I, umm, I can take you to the farm. It not far."

"Where is it?"

She pointed over Laura's shoulder. "Two hours walk that way."

Laura felt her chest tighten slightly at the realization they were in the middle of nowhere, this location clearly chosen for the fact it was a crossroads that led to the resort. She glanced around, no vehicles in sight beyond their own. "You walk here?"

"Every day." Florence shrugged. "It okay. It let me think."

Laura glanced at James, and she could see in his eyes how affected he was by their few minutes with this young woman. She smiled at Florence, patting her hand again. "Aren't you simply wonderful. Can you take us there?"

Florence nodded as the food arrived, the aroma intoxicating. They were all eager to pursue the mystery they had discovered last night, though the wide eyes on Florence's face made the young woman's priorities clear.

"Umm, can we go after we eat?" She seemed ashamed to ask the question, the woman clearly starving.

Laura smiled. "Hungry?"

Florence shrugged, turning away slightly.

Laura patted her stomach. "Well, I am. Let's eat!"

Erasmus Farm

Outside Belfast, South Africa

"Welcome, welcome!" The old farmer, his hair a bright silver, his skin a dark leathery tan, exchanged handshakes with his new arrivals. "So many professors, I feel like I'm back at school!"

Acton smiled, the man extremely pleasant and so far accommodating despite their unannounced arrival. "Don't worry, there's no test, Mr. Erasmus."

The farmer tossed his head back, laughing. "Please, call me Marius. Now, what can I do for such distinguished guests?"

"Oddly enough, we're here to see Miss Mokoena's father, if it's possible. It shouldn't take long."

"Ahh, Bongani. One of my best workers, though he's getting up in age like I am!" He roared with laughter again. "He's a hard worker and a good father, hey Florence?"

"Yes, Mr. Erasmus," she murmured.

"What's your business with him?"

Laura held up the medallion, careful to show the side with the lioness. "I understand he makes these. I wanted to see if he could make me some more."

"Ahh, yes, he's quite the craftsman." He pointed to a nearby barn. "He should be in there, working on the tractor. She's acting up again, and only he seems to be able to fix it. Go ahead, and when you're done, come join the wife and I for some lemonade, we don't get many visitors around here and some good conversation would brighten an otherwise mundane day."

Acton's mouth watered at the prospect. "Thank you, we shouldn't be long." Florence led the way to the barn, apparently eager to see her father, though he had the slight sense she was nervous around the farmer. Though apartheid had been over for probably her entire lifetime, there seemed to be either distrust or fear in her demeanor, perhaps from knowing this man had complete control over her family as the employer of her father.

"Tata?"

The sounds of work inside the barn stopped. "Nunu?" They stepped inside, Acton's eyes taking a moment to adjust to the dramatically darker interior. A shirtless man in remarkable shape for being probably in his late fifties, pulled out from under a tractor equally as old. "What brings you here?" His eyes narrowed as he noticed she wasn't alone, quickly trying to make himself more presentable, his head bowing slightly. "Who are these people?"

"They are tourists from the lodge, Tata. I sold them the medallion you made me"—Laura held it out—"and they wanted to meet you."

His eyes narrowed further. "Why? Did she not charge you a fair price?"

Laura smiled, stepping forward and putting a hand on Florence's shoulder. "Oh, that's not it at all. Your daughter has been an absolute delight. She's a fine young woman, a testament to you."

He relaxed slightly, batting the compliment away. "She takes after her mother, a far finer person than me." He looked about, grabbing his shirt off a nearby bench, shrugging it on. "Now what is it you want? I'm quite busy."

Laura held out the medallion again. "You made this?"

A quick nod.

"Can you tell us how?"

Again, the eyes narrowed. "Why? If you want more, I'll make them for you. I'm not going to let you copy them and cheat me out of money. I need that to feed my family."

Laura shook her head, holding out her hands. "Oh no, we have no intention of doing that. We'll happily pay you for showing us how you make them."

"Money first."

"Tata!"

He held out a finger, cutting her off. "Stay out of this, little one, this is business."

Florence crossed her arms, a pout expressing her displeasure as Acton pulled out a money clip, peeling off several bills. He handed them over. "Is that enough?"

Bongani quickly took the bills, fingering through them then giving them a sniff, as if he wasn't sure whether they were real. He counted them again, his eyes returning to Acton's hands, still holding the clip.

Acton smiled, thumbing over a few more. "Now I think you're taking advantage of us."

"Tata!"

Bongani grunted, shoving the bills in his pocket before spinning on his heel and walking deeper into the barn. He pointed at an old anvil and a large hammer. "I use this." He pointed at a pile of scrap metal. "I use the old metal, hammer out the shape, trim it, file it, punch a hole, put a string."

Florence raised her hand, eager to share. "I make the string."

Laura beamed a smile at her, stepping closer to the small workshop. "But how do you make the engravings?"

Bongani pointed at an old, ornate piece of metal, something that might have once occupied a prominent place in a home, there half a dozen intricate, thumb-sized carvings in the strip of what might be iron. "I use that. It's harder than the tin I use, so I just hammer on it and it takes the shape."

Laura nodded, appreciating the ingenuity. She flipped over the medallion. "And this side?"

The old man pulled a large coin from his pocket, placing it on the anvil. "I use this to size it." He grabbed a piece of tin from the pile, placing it over the coin, then hammered down on it several times with the mallet. The pliable metal quickly took the shape of the coin, the hammer soon tossed aside, tinsnips cutting around the circular indentation. He handed it over, shoving the coin in his pocket. "Careful, it's still sharp."

Laura flipped it over, everyone gathering around, Acton exchanging an excited grin with his wife. There was no doubt. It matched her medallion exactly.

And the photos from the Smithsonian's staff website.

He gestured to Bongani's pocket. "May I see the coin?"

Bongani shrugged, handing it over. Acton held it up to a shaft of light piercing the old roof overhead. "Am I seeing what I think I'm seeing?"

Gorman's eyes were wide. "I think so!"

Acton looked at the others, his heart pounding. "My God, could we have just found the missing Kruger Gold?"

Outside Belfast, South African Republic
May 3rd, 1900

It was suffocating, and it was definitely disgraceful, the shame of it overwhelming. Voorneveld was tempted to shove the corpse of his friend and commanding officer off him, and confront the British soldiers picking through the bodies of his men, searching for prisoners. Yet he resisted.

On any other day, he would have gone down fighting.

Though not today.

Today he had to somehow survive.

His men had fought bravely, but they were overwhelmingly outnumbered, yet despite that, he was certain they had taken four or five of the enemy for every one of them. They could have surrendered, they could have survived, but they all knew the secret they possessed had to be preserved, or their nation's future would be lost.

In the final moments of the battle, he had hidden under his friend, hoping to survive the encounter so he could return to Pretoria and inform Command of where the gold was hidden. He was willing to die—it was something he didn't fear—yet no one but he knew where the gold was hidden beyond a simple though loyal farmer, who could die tomorrow should the British suspect anything.

"There's two more over here."

He took a deep breath, preparing for what was to come, trying to relax every muscle in his body as he lay on his stomach, face in the dirt, praying they wouldn't pay him any mind. His pistol was tucked under him, gripped in his hand and ready to fire, though not at the British scum, its bullet reserved for himself, there no way he would be taken alive, no way he'd be forced to give up the country's most important secret.

He felt his friend's body roll off his back, slapping unceremoniously on the ground beside him.

"Bloody hell, this one's head is almost gone."

"Check the other one. I don't see a wound."

He was grabbed by the shoulder and flipped over, but he didn't move a muscle, the blood and dirt he had smeared over his face hopefully enough to disguise the fact he was probably turning red from holding his breath.

"Hey, look, he's still holding his gun."

"Take it."

He heard the soldier moving, then exhaled with a grunt as what must have been a knee shoved into his stomach.

"Bloody hell, he's alive!"

The pressure was relieved as the soldier jumped back, Voorneveld opening his eyes, several guns pointed directly at him.

"Don't shoot him, we need prisoners otherwise we'll never find where they hid it."

And at that moment Voorneveld realized his suspicions had been right all along. They had been betrayed. By whom, it didn't matter, though the fact it had happened was now obvious.

And his duty was clear.

He glared at the British officer, then a sense of calm swept over him. He smiled, eliciting confusion from his would-be captors. He whipped the gun from his chest and pressed it against his temple.

"For my home."

Erasmus Farm

Outside Belfast, South Africa

Present Day

Acton held up the coin. "Are there more of these?"

Bongani shrugged. "Don't know." His eyes narrowed. "You said Kruger Gold. I've heard of that. Is it valuable?"

Acton smiled. "In the right hands."

"You mean yours."

"Frankly, yes. We're teachers, not treasure hunters. If you help us, I'll personally make sure you're rewarded." Acton tilted his head toward Florence. "You'll be able to take care of your family. Forever."

Bongani's eyes widened.

"Where did you find it?" asked Laura, Acton sensing she was trying to hide her excitement. And failing miserably.

"On the farm."

Everyone exchanged glances. Acton held out an arm, pointing toward the door. "Show us where!"

Bongani shook his head. "I have to fix the tractor first. It's more important."

"But—"

He peeled off his shirt and tossed it back on the bench. "If I don't get it working, then we have to do everything by hand. Many sore backs." He gestured for them to leave. "Don't worry, when my work is over, I'll show you. It's not going anywhere. A few more hours won't change that."

Acton suppressed his frustration, forcing a smile. He bowed slightly. "You're right of course. Your job must come first." He motioned for the others to leave. "We'll leave you to your work."

Bongani grunted, diving under the tractor once again, Florence appearing aghast at what had happened, her eyes conveying her apologies to Acton and Laura. Laura put an arm around her as they left the barn.

"I'm so sorry. Once he starts working on something, he never wants to stop."

Laura squeezed the young woman's shoulders. "It's okay, we're patient people. And your father is right. His job must come first. How about we go have that lemonade?"

"Oh, I, umm, shouldn't. It wouldn't be right."

"Hello!" called Marius from the veranda that graced the entire front of the farmhouse, his wife appearing with a tray containing a large pitcher and several glasses. Acton waved at him with a smile, turning back to Florence, understanding exactly why she wouldn't want to sit with her father's boss.

"Would you like Sipho to take you home, or back to your store?"

She nodded, though turned away slightly, clearly ashamed to ask for any favors. Acton looked at Sipho who smiled eagerly.

"Mr. Professor, sir, I can drop her off, then if I may, might I take the opportunity to visit my brother? He lives near here and I haven't seen him in a long time."

Acton smiled as they reached the veranda, the problem solved. "Absolutely. Drop her off wherever she wants, visit your brother, then come pick us up." He turned to the farmer. "That is, of course, if you don't mind."

The old farmer brushed off the suggestion he might. "Of course! You can keep us company. Like I said, we rarely get visitors."

Sipho grinned, heading quickly for the Toyota with Florence as those that remained took seats on the veranda, Acton giving everyone a slight look to make sure they understood nothing was to be said.

It was unnecessary.

Introductions were made once again for the benefit of Marius' wife, Rina, then lemonade was poured, thirsts quenched, Acton letting out a satisfied sigh after his first large gulp. "Delicious."

Rina beamed. "Thank you. Old family recipe." She put down her glass. "So you're all professors?"

Angeline shook her head. "I'm not, but the rest of them are." She smiled. "Can't say I ever took enough of a liking to school to stay any longer than I had to." She took a sip. "I met Gorman when I was seventeen, and we've been together ever since. I stayed home to raise our five children."

"Five! That's a handful!"

Angeline agreed with a contented smile. "Definitely." She glanced at the large house then at Rina. "Do you have children?"

Rina frowned, her husband reaching out and taking her hand. "I…"

"We weren't able to have children," finished Marius.

Angeline was aghast. "Oh, I'm so sorry, I shouldn't have—"

"Nonsense!" cried Marius. "How could you have known? And it's a perfectly reasonable question. Besides, we have lots of nieces and nephews that we're close to, and they bring their children around now, so we get to spoil them."

"That's good." Acton put his already half-empty glass down. "Family is important." He reached out and squeezed Laura's hand. "We can't have children either."

"You poor dear." Rina patted Laura on the arm. "Don't you worry, you'll get used to the idea and find other ways to fill your life."

Laura's eyes glistened and she nodded, saying nothing. Acton squeezed her hand tighter, both still getting used to the idea that they'd never have children of their own. But Rina was right, there were other ways to fill their lives, and for now, it was their careers and the students that came with that.

They'd be fine.

It would just take time.

Gorman apparently sensed a need to change the subject. He held up his glass. "This is excellent. You can tell you have a practiced hand."

Rina smiled. "Thank you. More?"

Gorman nodded, Rina quickly refilling his glass. He pointed at a tin sign over the front door, Acton turning, noticing it for the first time. "Swart. That sounds familiar. Where do I know it from?"

Marius smiled. "It depends on how well you know your Boer War."

Acton's eyebrows leaped as he leaned forward. "We're all professors of archaeology and history here. I think you just got our attention."

Marius laughed. "Well, let me tell you a story."

Outside Belfast, South African Republic
May 3rd, 1900

Boet Swart climbed down from his horse at the end of the long dirt road that led to his farm, the crossroads now a horror. Should he ever need to picture what Hades must be, he was now privy to the imagery, a repulsive sight he had little doubt he'd ever forget.

He eyed the horizon warily, no one in sight, as he quickly checked the faces of the fallen commandos, his chest tightening as he recognized those who had arrived at his farm earlier in the day. He paused as he spotted the young veldkornet leading the small team that had buried the state's gold on his property. He removed his hat, placing it over his heart as he said a silent prayer for the man's soul, it clear he had taken his own life.

Forgive him, Lord, for he did it not for selfish reasons, but for the greater good.

He climbed back on his horse, wondering what he should do, it evident no one in Pretoria knew where the gold was now hidden, the secret entrusted to his family only hours before, taking on a critical new nature.

A horse whinnied in the distance and he spun in his saddle, cursing as half a dozen British soldiers cleared the rise. He turned his horse, urging it back toward the farm, hoping he hadn't been seen, but a frantic glance over his shoulder had his heart pounding, they clearly in pursuit. As he jumped the short fence at the front of the property, he shouted to the workers in the fields to run. Confused, their questions were all answered when they spotted the British. Screams erupted and the dozens of innocent souls dropped their implements, rushing in the opposite direction, his daughters and wife running into the farmhouse as he arrived. They emerged moments later, all armed, his eldest, Mitzi, tossing him a rifle as he smacked his horse's hindquarters, sending it toward the barn.

He turned to his family. "Inside, now!"

They obeyed, the door closing behind them as he turned to face the arriving British, his gun held casually at his side, available to him with a quick pop of his forearm.

"Lower your weapon!"

Swart glanced down at it. "It *is* lowered."

The officer in charge, too young for such an honor in Swart's opinion, glared at him as all six horses lined up neatly. "You dare defy an officer of the British Empire?"

"I'm not defying anyone. I'm on my farm, my property. How may I assist you?"

"Why did you run?"

Swart shrugged. "Wouldn't you?"

"Where do your loyalties lie?" The question was asked as if there was only one correct answer.

"To God."

"Not your Queen?"

"As far as I'm aware, the South African Republic has no queen."

A sneer emerged on the soldier's face. "So you acknowledge you are a combatant, an enemy of the Empire."

Swart shook his head, raising his forearm slightly. "I said no such thing. I am a farmer, a husband, and a father. I take no sides in this battle between your queen and Oom Paul Kruger. When this is all finished with, and you have won, or he has won, my farm will remain. Should I be left alone until then, I will reap what I sow, sell it to the highest bidder, and continue on with my life, never having fired a shot in a war that does not concern me."

The officer keyed off something he said, rising in his saddle and turning toward the fields filled with crops ready to harvest. He sat back down. "Burn it."

Smiles spread across the soldiers' faces as Swart stepped forward. "No! You can't! I've done nothing wrong!"

"You're Boer scum who aimed a weapon at Her Majesty's forces. You're lucky I don't have you all lined up and shot!"

A torch was lit then used to light several others as Swart slowly backed away, his forearm rising a little more.

"I suggest you get your family out of your house while you can."

Swart turned his back on the soldiers, his eyes sweeping from left to right across the veranda, spotting the shadow of his wife standing to the side of one of the windows, his daughters at the others.

And knew what he had to do.

He had to protect his family's future, like those brave commandos had protected their nation's.

He spun, firing his rifle, blasting the smug officer off his perch, then tossed it aside as he pulled the revolver from his belt. The windows on either side burst open, the brave women of his family opening fire on the remaining soldiers, the British dropping within seconds, only one avoiding a hit in the initial volley. He spun his horse around and urged it forward as a rifle was tossed through the window to Swart who caught it, taking careful aim.

He fired.

And the last of those who would have destroyed all his family had worked for generations to create, fell to the lead of his rifle.

Swart strode from the veranda, his wife and daughters stepping through the door, and checked for survivors. The officer moaned and Swart stood beside him, aiming his pistol at the man's head.

"You'll pay for this."

Swart frowned. "I already have. With my soul." He squeezed the trigger.

Sealing his fate.

Erasmus Farm

Outside Belfast, South Africa

Present Day

Marius pointed to the end of the long drive. "A famous battle, at least among the locals and treasure hunters, took place at the end of that road."

Acton played only slightly dumb. "Treasure hunters? As in Kruger's Gold?"

Marius' head bobbed, apparently impressed. "Exactly. I see you know your history."

Acton grinned. "I know my Lethal Weapon movies."

Marius stared at him, puzzled for a moment, before he made the connection, tossing his head back and delivering a robust belly laugh. "Yes, yes, of course. Lethal Weapon Two was a good laugh."

"Where's the pool?" said Rina in her best Mel Gibson voice.

"No pool. This house is built on stilts!"

Everyone laughed, Acton making a mental note to have a Lethal Weapon marathon when they got back home, and toss in Get the Gringo for good measure.

Marius calmed himself, taking a sip of his lemonade. "But, as a good historian, you should know that those were Krugerrands, which are different than the Kruger Gold."

Acton nodded. "Yes, of course. Krugerrands were minted starting in the sixties, weren't they? Named after Paul Kruger, but not related to the gold actually ordered moved by him during the Second Boer War."

"Exactly."

"So you're saying that something happened here on this farm, something related to the missing Kruger Gold?"

Marius beamed as if he were responsible for the entire event. "Yes! The rumor is that the gold came through here, but they were ambushed." He pointed to the road. "Down there, at the crossroads. Some escaped, buried the gold, then returned to help their comrades. They all died, so no one knew where they had buried it."

Acton knew the story of how the gold had been lost, and also realized it was in this general vicinity, as in knowing that the Battle of Gettysburg took place in Pennsylvania. He had no idea they were a mile from the battle. "Very interesting."

"Bah, that's nothing. Here's the interesting part. My grandmother, on her deathbed, said something to my father that I will never forget. She said that the stories of the buried gold were true, and that it had been buried here, on this very farm."

Acton's heart raced and he resisted the urge to share the excitement with the others lest their real reason for being there be revealed. "I assume your father looked."

Marius shook his head. "No, it was the ramblings of an old woman whose faculties had long since left her. She also claimed they moved the gold after she killed some British soldiers during the war. She said they buried the bodies in the same hole where the gold had been." He sighed. "I hope they find a cure for dementia one of these days. No one should have to go like that." He patted his wife's leg. "I've told Rina to shoot me if I ever get that way."

"He has." She winked. "And I will."

Marius laughed. "And I have no doubt you will." He leaned toward Acton. "A few times I think she was ready to try a little early. Usually when I get into the drink a little too much."

"You say the stupidest things when you're drunk. It's easy to mistake it."

More laughter from around the table gave Acton a chance to exchange a brief, excited glance with Laura before a wave of concern swept over him.

Did he say they moved *the gold?*

Tladi Tsabalala Residence

Belfast, South Africa

"Where is he?" asked Sipho as he exchanged a quick embrace with his brother's wife.

"In the shed."

Sipho let her go, frowning. "What's he up to now?"

She shook her head, returning to the pot on the stove. "I never ask. As long as he puts food on the table, I don't care."

"You'll care if he gets himself killed."

She gave him a look that suggested she wouldn't.

And he didn't blame her.

Tladi wasn't a good man. He had been committing petty crimes since he was old enough to run, and he habitually fell in with the wrong crowds, no matter how many times his elder brother helped him.

And he beat his wife.

Unforgivable.

Sipho walked through the house, coming out the back. He rapped on the corrugated metal siding that made up the frame of the shed, and walked inside. His brother spun toward him then grabbed a tarp, tossing it over a pile of something in the back, Sipho's eyes not yet having had time to adjust.

"What is that?" He asked the question, though the stench had already given him the answer.

His brother looked at him. "What is what?"

Sipho pointed at the tarp. "That!" He leaned in, something poking out the bottom. "That looks like elephant tusks! Ivory!"

His brother stepped between him and the pile. "So what if it is?"

"So what if it is? It's illegal, that's what!"

"Pfft. Only if I'm caught."

Sipho shook his head. "What would father say if he saw you now, a poacher?"

Tladi grinned. "He'd say, 'where's my cut?'"

Sipho frowned. "You have a very shameful opinion of our father."

"Yeah, well, where is he now? Gone!"

"He's dead, not gone. Hardly his fault."

"That's what you say. I think he just left us, and mother is lying."

Sipho shook his head, sighing. "You're too young to remember. *I* do. *I* was there."

"So *you* say."

Sipho stepped toward his brother, eyes narrowed. "Are you calling me a liar?"

Tladi backed off slightly, Sipho still the eldest. "No, no." He pointed at the tarp-covered pile. "This will change our lives. All our lives. You won't need to ferry rich white people around to look at animals, pretending to be happy about it, fulfilling their every wish."

Sipho crossed his arms. "It's not like that. I like my job."

"Bullshit. No one could like a job like that. Yes, sir, no sir, right away, sir. You're like their slave."

Sipho felt his chest tighten. "How would you know? You've never worked a day in your life."

"I work, brother, I work." He pointed again at the pile. "That's months of work."

Sipho noted the size of the pile, disturbingly large. "And how many innocent, endangered animals had to die?"

Tladi shrugged. "Who cares? They're just animals. I'm human, and I'm hungry. If poaching wasn't illegal, I'd stick around and eat them after I shot them. Hell, if they'd just let us farm the damned things, we'd have an endless supply of ivory and there'd be no need for what I do."

"That will never happen."

Tladi jabbed the air between them. "Exactly, which is why I poach."

"Bullshit, you'd still do it even if they allowed farming. You've always had a problem with authority."

Tladi shrugged. "Maybe if father hadn't run out on us, I'd be a better man, like you."

Sipho shook his head. "I'm done with this conversation. I just came to say hello, and instead I find out you're even more of a criminal than before, and you continue to insult our father." He stormed from the shed, walking down the side of the house rather than return inside, his brother on his heels.

"You're right, brother. I'm sorry."

Sipho paused, turning to face his younger sibling.

"Look, I'm a fool, not like my wiser older brother." He jerked a thumb over his shoulder. "Forget what you saw. Let this be a happy occasion. It's been so long since I've seen you. What brings you here?"

Sipho let out a slow breath, forcing a smile. His brother would never change, but he was family. Blood. And that had to count for something. "Some professors I'm guiding are visiting the Erasmus farm."

"Oh yeah, why?"

Sipho shrugged. "Not sure. Some medallion they bought got them all excited."

Tladi's eyes narrowed. "Medallion? Valuable?"

Sipho shook his head. "Don't get any ideas, little brother. It's made of tin and they only paid a few rand for it."

"How would you know?"

"I was there when they bought it. From Florence, you know, who runs the little souvenir stand. Her father makes them."

Tladi's head bobbed slowly. "Oh yeah, I know her. Pretty girl."

Sipho pointed at the house. "You've got a pretty wife in there."

Tladi glanced over his shoulder and shrugged. "Yeah, well, listen, brother. I'm kind of busy. How about you come visit me another time."

Sipho sensed his brother was trying to get rid of him. His eyes narrowed. "What are you up to, brother?"

"Nothing. At least nothing you want to know about."

Sipho sighed. "Please, for mother's sake if you won't do it for father, stop the poaching. You're going to get yourself killed. Then who will take care of your family?"

A broad smile spread across Tladi's face. "You will, and you won't have to worry about your little brother anymore."

Swart Farm

Outside Belfast, South African Republic

May 4th, 1900

"Make sure the hole is deep. They can't ever be found."

Swart's young daughters looked up at him, both echoing their reply. "Yes, Papa."

He glanced over at the two carts, loaded with the gold that had been buried earlier in the day. From the moment the gunfire had stopped, they had been working, loading the bodies of the dead soldiers into a cart and hauling it to the back of the property where the commandos had hidden the gold. They had dug it up, loading it into their carts, the precious metal deceptively heavy.

It had taken the entire day and most of the night, backbreaking work that had his body weakened by the effort. He sat down, gasping for air as his wife held a ladle of water to his mouth. He drank it thirstily, smiling his thanks.

"Are you okay? You don't seem well."

"Just a tiring day. I'll be fine once this is finished."

"We should have just taken them to the battle site and left them there."

He shook his head. "Like I said before, they had already taken their dead. If they found six fresh bodies, they'd know somebody in the area had killed them. They'd burn us all out."

His wife frowned, unconvinced. "They're still going to know they're missing."

He took another drink. "Yes, but Mitzi's taking care of their horses. If we're lucky, they'll think they were deserters, or were ambushed nowhere near here."

His wife frowned, staring in the direction Mitzi had left in hours before. "I hope she's okay."

He patted his wife's hand. "She will be. She's a smart girl, that one."

"Done, Papa!"

He pushed himself to his feet, surveying the expanded hole and nodded his approval. "Excellent work, girls. Now let's hurry up and finish this. It will be light before you know it."

Florence Mokoena Residence

Belfast, South Africa

Present Day

Florence hummed, as happy as she had been in a long time. She was home now, having had Sipho drop her off at the market, rewarding herself by using some of the extra money the generous tourists had given her, to buy additional food.

They would eat well tonight.

No hungry tummies before bedtime.

She wondered what it must be like to be white and rich. It had to be good. It was something she would never know, and like her late husband had said, something to not even bother thinking about.

Why wish for something that can never be?

She grunted as her knife expertly worked the soet patate, one of her favorite root vegetables. She could never be white, therefore she could never be rich.

Her late husband's voice echoed in her head.

You don't need to be white to be rich.

But he was a dreamer. She paused, picturing the four tourists who had changed her family's day. Two whites, two blacks.

Maybe he's right. But it definitely helps.

She frowned as she remembered the four young people and how mean they were to her.

If that's what being rich means, then I don't want to be rich.

She sighed, staring at the only photo she had of her beloved, hung on the wall of their small two-room house. He had died in a farming accident, kicked in the head by a skittish horse. It was a freak occurrence that never should have happened.

Yet it had.

And it had changed their lives forever, all their plans destroyed, visions of a future together swept away in an instant, two weeks wages her compensation, the envelope a finger in the bursting dam of hardships that would follow.

If she had thought their humble life before was hard, nothing had prepared her for this.

Her father had stepped up as she knew he would, he a good man. Her mother was long dead, but he had taken over as the breadwinner for her and her children without hesitation.

And it was breaking him.

He took every bit of extra work offered at the farm or in town, Mr. Erasmus, privy to the situation, was generous but only to a point, he not a charitable man—extra money meant extra work, though sometimes the work wasn't necessarily urgent, only offered to help.

She understood. If Mr. Erasmus just gave money, everyone would have their hand out. When her father's friend, who ran the paap 'n vleis stand outside the park, had seen the scarf she was wearing, he had asked her where she had bought it. When he heard she made it, he had been immediately interested, offering her money to make more.

And the souvenir stand had been born.

She made her scarves and various other crafts, her father hammering out medallions when he could find the time, and it had allowed her to contribute to their situation, though barely. Today was the exception, rather than the norm, selling out her entire supply. It would feed them for a week at least, perhaps giving her poor father a rest.

She closed her eyes, saying a silent prayer of thanks.

A hard rap at the door startled her.

She put down her knife and opened the door, gasping. "Tladi, what are you doing here?"

He stepped inside without an invite, his puffed out chest causing her to step back from the door. He closed it behind him and her heart leaped into her throat.

"You and I need to talk."

Her eyes were wide, the blood pounding in her ears. "Wh-what about?"

"About that medallion you sold my brother's keepers.

South of Belfast, South African Republic

May 4th, 1900

Mitzi's heart had been hammering hard for hours now, running on pure adrenaline. If she slowed down, she'd probably run out of steam and fall asleep in her saddle. But she had no choice, her poor horse, Alexander, pushed too hard for too long, now needing a rest.

Yet it had been necessary.

The soldiers' horses needed to be moved as far from the family farm as possible. Her father was ill, something he didn't know she was aware of. He would never have been able to undertake the journey, and if anything were to happen to him, the entire family would be helpless. Her mother was needed to take care of her father and her younger sisters, leaving the task to her, the eldest.

Under normal circumstances, they could have asked any one of the relatives on a nearby farm for help, but with the secret entrusted her family, and the fact they had killed six British soldiers, they couldn't risk bringing anyone else in on their sins and their sworn duty.

That, again, left her.

It was dark, the only light from the stars and moon above, though it was enough for her to know exactly where she was, which was about as far as she had ever ventured from her home—certainly the farthest she had been on her own. It was as exciting as it was terrifying, and though she desperately wished she weren't here, she also felt more like a grown woman today than at any time of her life.

She was saving her family, as her mother would have should she not have a daughter old enough to fulfill the duty, and should she die here today, she would be remembered as having died a woman, not a little girl.

And it made her proud.

A horse whinnied ahead and her heart slammed, her feelings of pride and womanhood shoved aside by the little girl that still dwelled inside.

Okay, calm down, you know what to say.

She should. She had rehearsed it over and over for hours. She urged her horse forward at a casual gait, the others following nonchalantly behind her, soon spotting several silhouettes ahead, clearly soldiers on horseback.

Soldiers who had spotted her, the sounds of their weapons being readied reaching her ears.

"Halt, who goes there?"

She recognized the accent.

British.

"A loyal subject of the Empire!"

"Advance and be recognized!"

She clicked, Alexander, who had been with her for years, reading her wishes perfectly, sauntering forward. One of the soldiers held up a lantern, highlighting them more than her.

"Gentlemen, are you British?"

"Aye."

"Thank God! I was afraid I'd run into those filthy Boers."

Someone chuckled. "Not bloody likely, not after the pasting we gave them earlier."

She forced a smile on her face. "I found these horses wandering near my cousin's property. I thought I should return them to you." She held out the reins, one of the soldiers dismounting. He examined the horses. "They're ours." He looked up at her as he took the reins. "Where did you say you found them?"

"About ten miles back, grazing. I didn't see their riders. Perhaps they were in your skirmish earlier? I do hope their masters are well."

"Perhaps." He stared up at her, one of the others approaching, holding the lantern higher, a glow cast over her now. "Aye, now you're a bonny lass, aren't you!" She didn't like the look of the smile that spread across his face. "What is a young one like you doing out at this time of night?"

Mitzi inhaled deeply, steadying herself. "My duty for Queen and country."

"Aye, that's a good lass. Perhaps you would like to join us, entertain the lads for a while."

She laughed, tossing her hair. "Oh, for shame! What kind of girl do you take me for?" She turned her horse around, blowing them a kiss. "I must get back, otherwise my father will be horribly cross." She urged her steed forward, at a reasonable pace, enough to take her away quickly, but not enough to imply flight.

"Come back, lass, we'll have a good time!"

She waved, continuing forward, their calls fading into the night, and once gone, her body finally betrayed her, shaking like the leaves on the nearby knob thorn trees.

She passed out, asleep within moments, her body draped over Alexander's neck, confident the trusted animal would find his own way home.

Erasmus Farm

Outside Belfast, South Africa

"You're sure this is where you found it?"

Bongani nodded vigorously at Acton's question, pointing at the professor's feet. "Yes, right there."

"Just the one?"

"Yes, when I was plowing last year, I saw something in the sun. I stopped and found it."

Acton turned to the farmer, they unable to keep the secret from him once they returned. "We'd like to do some digging here, if you don't mind."

The old man shrugged. "Suit yourself. You won't find anything, but if you do, it's mine."

Acton bit his tongue. "Of course, you'll receive full credit."

Marius smiled at him, knowing full-well what Acton's carefully chosen words meant. "I don't take credit, I take cash!" He roared with laughter, his head tossed back once again, hands on the sides of his stomach. "Get it?" He turned, strolling back toward the farmhouse. "Oh, that's a good one. I have to tell Rina that one."

Acton chuckled, happy it had gone so well, there a distinct possibility Marius could have ordered them off the property, only to dig for the gold once they were gone.

He clearly believes there's nothing here.

He looked at the others, everyone with shovels, picks and various other tools of the trade. "Ready to dig?"

Laura grinned. "Oh yeah, let's get at it!"

And they dug.

And dug.

Each test hole, four feet apart, four feet deep, coming up empty, Acton fearing they might have to go even further down, perhaps the coin a stray that had somehow managed to work its way to the surface from far deeper.

Or perhaps Bongani's memory wasn't what it once was, and they were nowhere near the right spot.

Laura squealed. "I have something!" She held her phone out over the hole, taking a photo, the flash illuminating the depths briefly in the sinking late afternoon sunlight. She checked the photo and grinned, handing it to her husband.

Acton joined in on the grinning. "Definitely something." He passed the phone to Gorman. "What do you think that is?"

Gorman pursed his lips, showing the phone to his wife. "If I had to hazard a guess, I'd say it's a human jawbone."

Swart Farm

Outside Belfast, South African Republic

May 4th, 1900

A whiney and gentle toss of the head had Alexander waking her. Mitzi sat up in her saddle, stretching, her foggy brain taking a moment to reorient, not entirely sure where she was or why she was there.

Then she remembered, a surge of adrenaline jolting her wide-awake. She looked about and breathed a sigh of relief, recognizing the family farm ahead. She urged Alexander on and was soon at the veranda, tying him to the post. She gently patted the side of his face. "Good boy." She gave him a hug and a kiss then stepped inside the house to find everyone sitting at the kitchen table.

Everyone except her father.

Her mother leaped to her feet, rushing toward her, arms extended. "Oh, thank the Lord! I had thought the worst!" She hugged her, hard, then pushed her toward her usual chair, grabbing bread and butter from the counter and shoving it in front of her, followed by a pitcher of milk. "What happened?"

Mitzi hadn't realized how hungry she was until she caught sight of the food. She attacked it, her younger sisters giggling. She covered her mouth, deciding she better answer her mother. "I handed them over to British soldiers about twenty miles from here."

Her mother's jaw dropped. "You did what!"

Mitzi shrugged, fighting the urge to resume shaking, the recollection of her deeds of last night also bringing back the fears. "It seemed the thing to do."

Her mother rounded the table and hugged her hard. "Oh, my brave, brave girl." She stepped back. "And my stupid girl! Didn't they question you? Ask you who you were?"

Mitzi swallowed. "They seemed more interested in my bodice than my pedigree."

Her mother smiled, patting her on the shoulder, surveying her girls. "Good thing I didn't have boys, then."

Mitzi downed her glass of milk, her mother pouring another. "Did you bury the soldiers?"

"Yes."

"Where's father?"

"He's moving the gold."

Mitzi paused. "To where?"

"He didn't say." Her mother sat down. "He said it's best we don't know."

"But what if Pretoria comes looking for it?"

"Then he'll tell them where it is."

"And if the British kill us first? What will our troops find in the hole?"

Her mother patted her hand. "Dead British soldiers, and, according to your father, a clue only a local could understand."

Somewhere over the Mediterranean Sea

Present Day

Dawson frowned as he fired off another text message to Maggie, his third with no response. He was concerned. It was now morning in Bragg and she had said she was staying in for the night, it not like her to go out on the town without letting him know, and unheard of since the incident in Paris.

Maybe she just fell asleep early.

It wouldn't be the first time, and normally he wouldn't worry too much about it, though he had a feeling she was hiding something from him. He wasn't a fool. He had noticed her massaging her hand over the past couple of days, and she had dropped a couple of things besides the glass yesterday, something completely out of character for her.

And he knew something was bothering her, able to read her better than she realized, though he hadn't pressed her, she probably not wanting to worry him.

That meant it was serious.

It has to be the head wound.

The doctors had said it could take years to fully recover, and they weren't sure if there would be any permanent complications, though so far she had been remarkably lucky, so much so, that now with her hair having grown back enough, it was easy to forget how close to death she had come in Paris. He pursed his lips.

"What's wrong?"

He glanced over at Niner, sitting across from him. "I can't reach Maggie."

Niner checked his watch. "Probably still asleep."

"Probably." He debated asking the question for a moment, then went ahead. After all, these were his brothers. There were no secrets between them, not with what they had been through. "Have you noticed anything with her lately?"

Niner gave him a look. "Dude, you're talking to the wrong guy. You mean, is she cheating on you?"

Dawson cocked an eye at him.

Niner waved off the question. "Sorry, you're right, who would ever cheat on the ultimate male."

"That's better."

Niner wiped a finger across his forehead, wicking away the imaginary sweat.

"No, I meant healthwise."

Niner shrugged, serious again. "Well, nothing outside of the usual."

Dawson's eyes narrowed, concerned. "What do you mean?"

Niner leaned forward, his voice gentle. "Well, BD, she's clearly got some sort of mental handicap to be engaged to a guy like you, but other than that, she seems completely normal."

Dawson chuckled, feigning a punch.

Niner frowned slightly as he regarded his friend. "You're serious, aren't you?"

Dawson nodded.

"Well, I'm the wrong guy to ask. I've been a little distracted myself, you know."

Dawson thought of the young Korean police officer that had worked with them recently, and how devastated Niner had been upon her death. "You good for the mission?"

"Yeah, I've made my peace." He leaned back in his seat. "Christ, I barely knew her, but still, well, you know."

Dawson definitely knew. "Yeah, I do." He smiled at his friend. "How about we kill some bad guys?"

Niner grinned. "That's exactly what I was thinking! I always feel better after we do that." He nodded at Dawson's cellphone, still gripped in his hand. "Why don't you have Red check on her if you're so concerned? Maybe Shirley can drop in on her?"

Dawson smiled, his head bobbing. "Good idea." He fired a text to his best friend, feeling a lot better.

Erasmus Farm

Outside Belfast, South Africa

Acton's expert eyes surveyed their dig, it the most excitement had on their vacation so far. Some might have said it was no longer a vacation, yet it was, this the most enjoyable thing he could think of doing—discovering history, solving a century-old puzzle, with the woman he loved at his side, and friends to share it with.

This vacation was to escape the bullets, bombs, terrorists, and cults.

It was perfect.

At this point, it wasn't clear how deep the graves had been originally, though after a century of nature taking its course, they were now about four feet below the surface. Six bodies lay piled atop each other, intermixed with remnants of British uniforms, period specific weapons and gear buried with them.

Laura stretched. "This was no formal burial."

Gorman agreed, the man having forgotten his earlier complaints of being too old to dig, now on his hands and knees with the rest of them. "It looks like they were hiding the bodies." He glanced up at Acton. "Didn't he say his grandmother talked of burying British soldiers?"

Acton nodded. "It would seem she was right." He smiled. "And that means the gold could have been buried here." He frowned, searching the hole. "But I don't see it, so maybe she was right about that too and they moved it."

Angeline held something up in the air. "You mean this gold?"

All lights pointed toward her hand, a dirt-covered object, about the size and shape of Bongani's gold coin, held triumphantly for all to see.

Her husband took the coin, giving her a kiss. "Have you been holding out on us?"

"No, evidently just showing you so-called archaeologists how it's done."

Laura laughed, climbing over to Angeline's side of the hole, pointing a flashlight at the ground, revealing several coins. "Looks like a small bundle here. Definitely no treasure trove, but...wait a minute, what's this?"

Everyone gathered closer as she pulled out a brush, removing the dirt from around what turned out to be the remnants of a broken jar, several coins in the bottom half.

"What's that?" asked Acton, pointing at what appeared to be a piece of cloth, wrapped around a small object.

Laura snapped several photos then carefully lifted it, Acton taking several more with his own phone before helping Laura out of the hole. She placed it on an unfolded piece of cloth Acton kept for such occasions, and carefully unwrapped the tiny bundle. Acton's eyes narrowed at what was revealed.

"What the hell is that?"

Northeast of Belfast, South African Republic
May 4th, 1900

A sudden spasm in his hip sent Swart to the ground, unable to move as he gasped for breath. He closed his eyes, staring out at the evening sun as he fought through the pain, a pain he had felt before.

But it was different this time.

This time, it *was* his time.

He pulled a flask from his pocket, unscrewing the cap and downing his self-prescribed painkiller, twisting the cap back on before returning it to what might be its final resting place. He looked about at the entrance to the old abandoned mine, wondering if this might be *his* final resting place. He removed the flask, downing another shot, resting it on his still heaving chest rather than returning it to his pocket. He stared down the shaft, satisfied with the job he had done, closing his eyes for a much-deserved rest.

The gold was safe from the British, his duty to his people complete.

It had taken two carts and four horses, but he had reached the site of the abandoned mine without being seen, then had taken all day to unload the gold and move it inside.

But his family was safe, the gold no longer on their farm.

He just wished there had been time to bury the soldiers somewhere else.

The fields were due to be plowed, and he knew his wife. She was a smart, capable woman, and she would make sure that section of the farm was plowed first, leaving no sign a hole had ever been dug.

There would be no evidence of their crime.

And his family would be safe.

I hope Mitzi made it home.

He frowned. It wasn't supposed to end like this, though he had known it was coming. He hadn't been well for months, if not longer. Something was eating away at him inside. He'd been coughing up blood, and had seen more when he went to the bathroom. Something was wrong, the pain now nearly constant, his appetite gone. Sores had begun to appear all over his body, to the point he hadn't bedded his wife for months now, lest she see his condition.

I wish I could have said goodbye.

A thought occurred to him and he reached into his pocket, retrieving a piece of paper and the fountain pen he had brought to leave a note with the treasure should it be found, thanking the good Lord he had been taught to read and write when he was a youngster. His pen hovered over the paper as he contemplated what to write.

What do you say to the woman you love, when you know she'll probably never get a chance to read it?

Erasmus Farm

Outside Belfast, South Africa

Present Day

"Looks like coal."

Acton agreed with Gorman's assessment. "But why would they wrap that?"

Laura rolled it gently in her hand, searching for anything that might give them a clue as to why someone had thought it special enough to preserve with a set of gold coins. His eyes popped wide open, as did hers.

"It's a clue!" they both cried simultaneously.

Gorman stared at them doubtfully. "You mean a clue as to where the actual gold is?"

Acton shrugged. "What else could it be?"

"It's a rock!"

Acton smiled, his friend exhausted and clearly skeptical. "Exactly, so if it's a clue, then it has to be the type of rock that's important."

Laura agreed. "It's coal, which is obviously fairly common, but it has to have some meaning. Perhaps it's meant to suggest a location?"

Gorman's doubts began to turn. "You mean like a mine?"

Laura jabbed the air between them. "Exactly!" She pulled out her phone, her thumbs flying over the screen, then frowned. "There're coal mines all over the country, though not in this immediate area."

Acton sat on a tarp, staring off into the distance as he puzzled out their clue. "It would have to have existed back then…" He snapped his fingers. "And be abandoned!"

Laura smiled, her eyes wide. "That's right, you wouldn't hide gold in an active mine."

Gorman's head bobbed. "That could make it difficult to find. It's been over a century. There isn't a person alive today who would have worked it."

Acton tapped his chin. "True, but whoever left this message knew about the mine, and must have assumed that locals would know about it. It was a secret message to those who would know the area intimately. They were trying to hide the gold from the British, sorry, hon"—he winked at his wife who shrugged—"so the message had to be obscure, otherwise whoever found the bodies and this jar with the coins in it would know immediately where to look. That's okay if it were Boers, but not Brits."

Gorman stared at him. "So what are you saying?"

"I'm saying we have to ask a local. Someone who knows the area, intimately."

"Okay, who? Mr. Erasmus?"

"Perhaps, but he knows why we're here. Can we trust that he'd tell us the truth?"

Laura nodded. "You're right. He could say he doesn't know where the mine is, then as soon as we leave, head over there and take the gold."

Gorman frowned. "Then who?"

Acton thought for a moment. "It has to be someone who doesn't know what we're looking for, and who knows the area like the back of their hand."

His eyes widened as he realized exactly who they had to ask, everyone turning toward the driveway at the far end of the property, their safari vehicle parked beside the farmer's pickup truck, Sipho sitting against one of the wheels.

Sometimes the answers just come to you.

Swart Farm

Outside Belfast, South African Republic

May 11th, 1900

Mitzi sat on the veranda, one of their cats in her lap, rocking on the chair her father would normally occupy for hours on end in the evening, watching the sun set on the farm. It had been a long week's work, but the crop had been harvested, the fields plowed, there no evidence left of the secrets they held.

And her father had yet to return.

And she knew, deep down, he never would.

He had rarely left the farm his grandfather had first planted over fifty years ago, so if he were taking the gold to some place he knew would be safe, it would be nearby.

Certainly no more than a day's ride.

It meant he had been captured, and if so, was likely dead.

She stopped rocking, her cat staring up at her.

Mother said there was a clue only a local would understand.

She fought the urge to rise, to grab a shovel and dig up that clue. To go find where he had hidden the gold and save her father from whatever fate had befallen him.

She sighed, her shoulders drooping as reality set in. It didn't matter where the gold was. If he had made it to the hiding place he would have hidden it and left, so going there would serve no purpose. And if he hadn't made it, he wouldn't be there regardless.

Tears burned her eyes as she imagined the worst.

They captured him, for certain!

Her shoulders heaved and she leaned forward, her cat leaping from her lap.

Oh father, why?

She stared up at the heavens, a silent prayer on her lips, hoping her father had died quickly and without pain. The cat rubbed against her legs, purring loudly, trying to comfort her, but the gesture went unnoticed as Mitzi continued to sob, her cries rolling over the empty fields her father had once worked, her sorrow wasted on the horrors of war and the tragedy that too often befell those asked to keep secrets greater than they should.

Maggie Harris Residence
Lake in the Pines Apartments, Fayetteville, North Carolina
Present Day

Shirley Belme knocked again, and again there was no answer. She could have kept knocking harder, but unlike their humble Married Quarters, this was an apartment with neighbors, many of whom were probably trying to sleep in on the weekend. When her husband had received the message from Dawson, she had begun making calls, no one in the network having seen Maggie. Her Facebook status showed her offline, her phone was going straight to voicemail, and her home phone went unanswered.

It was enough to get her in the car with the spare key to Dawson's place. From there she had retrieved his spare to Maggie's apartment, a key she now pushed into the lock, opening the door slightly, her heart pounding as she wasn't sure what she might find.

"Maggie? You home?"

Still nothing.

She pushed the door all the way open, noting that the chain wasn't on, suggesting Maggie either wasn't home, or if she was, was expecting someone with a key—and as far as Shirley knew, that would only be Dawson. She closed the door behind her, reaching for the wall switch, suddenly feeling insecure, the living room curtains obviously closed, leaving the apartment dark. The hallway flooded with light, nothing out of the ordinary visible, though that did little to calm her nerves.

"Maggie?"

She glanced to her left, the kitchen empty, there no evidence of an evening meal having been cooked.

Could she have gone out with friends?

She shook her head.

She'd be home by now. Unless she spent the night somewhere.

She paused. If she were spending the night at a friend's, she would have told Dawson.

Unless she didn't want him to know.

A pit formed in her stomach for a brief moment then was pushed aside as she dismissed the ridiculous notion. Maggie loved Dawson desperately, and there was no way she would cheat on him. Though she didn't know Maggie as well as she knew some of the other women in the family that was the Unit, they had become close over the past year when Maggie and Dawson had finally become a couple.

She was difficult to avoid, what with Dawson and her husband being best friends.

And she never avoided her. Maggie was a delight, and she clearly made Dawson happy, which was all that mattered to her and Red.

She flicked the living room lights on, again finding everything in perfect order, pressing deeper into the apartment with increasing speed, her desperation to find the missing woman growing. The bedroom was empty, the bed made, the bathroom empty, the shower floor dry.

Her heart pounded hard.

She fired a text message indicating her failure to the other wives who were searching Maggie's known haunts including her gym and yoga studio, and the ceramics class she took.

And all replied that they too had no luck finding her.

She slowly examined the apartment for clues, no longer searching for Maggie, but for any evidence of where she might have gone. As she retraced her steps, the bathroom to the bedroom, the living area to the hallway, she paused, staring at the table near the door, a ceramic bowl sitting there, empty, it where she knew from previous visits Maggie kept her keys.

And her security pass.

Her jaw slowly dropped.

If she had come home, then gone back out, she would have left the pass here.

She quickly looked around for a purse, finding none.

She never made it home!

She tried Maggie's cellphone one last time, and again it went directly to voicemail.

Something's definitely wrong.

Erasmus Farm

Outside Belfast, South Africa

Gorman secured the gold coins and the "clue" in the back of their vehicle, sealed in a backpack, away from curious eyes, as Acton distracted the farmer and his wife.

"So, waste of time?"

Acton shook his head, not needing to fake any of his excitement. "On the contrary! We found the bodies of several British soldiers." He gestured toward Gorman as he joined the group. "Professor Ncube will be contacting his university and they'll notify the proper authorities. I expect a team will arrive within the next couple of days to do a proper excavation."

Marius frowned, glancing at the rear of his farm. "I need to plant this field in the next week. They better be done by then."

Acton smiled. "They won't take up much space, and you can probably ask for some sort of compensation for your losses."

Marius grunted. "The last time Pretoria did anything right, I was a young man with a good hip and a flat belly." He slapped his prominent stomach before his eyes narrowed. "Did you find the gold?"

Acton laughed. "No such luck. Just some coins from a purse on one of the soldiers that had broken open. Pretty much worthless to anyone besides us archaeologists."

Marius sighed. "Too bad. I might have retired. I'm getting too old to work this farm, and without children"—he shrugged—"well, perhaps it's time to sell."

Acton felt for the man, and suddenly saw himself in twenty years. His lifestyle had him crawling all over hell's creation, and it was taking a toll on his body. Would he eventually be in constant pain from bad joints, cushioning his six-pack abs with a keg? He absentmindedly scratched his stomach.

Don't worry. With the luck you've been having lately, you won't live that long.

He extended his hand to the farmer. "Well, we're going to get back to our hotel. It's been a pleasure." He nodded toward the dig in the distance. "Hopefully we've given you something to talk about with your neighbors."

The old man's face brightened. "Yes, it would appear grandmother was telling the truth after all." He shrugged. "At least some of it." His eyes narrowed. "Maybe the gold *is* there, after all."

Acton desperately wanted to steer him away from the thought, but if he did, it might mean revealing their secret, a secret that must be kept. "Oh, I think if there was any gold here, it would have turned up long ago. If there were thousands of coins, surely some would have shown up by now."

Marius grunted, disappointment written on his face. "You're right, of course. Just the dreams of a tired old man." He led them to their vehicle, handshakes exchanged. "Good journey."

Acton smiled as Sipho started up the vehicle. "Thank you once again." Marius waved as they pulled away, Sipho turning the opposite direction from the way they had come, setting off alarm bells. "Umm, aren't we going the wrong way?"

Sipho glanced in his mirror. "No. That way is if you want to go for food. This way is direct to the lodge. It will save us some time."

Acton leaned back in his seat, smiling. "You're the expert."

"Thank you, Mr. Professor." Sipho stared in the rearview mirror. "A fruitful day?"

Acton nodded. "Very interesting. I think Professor Ncube's people will be busy for quite some time examining the find."

"What did you find?"

"Just the bodies of some British soldiers from the Boer War."

"Oh." Sipho sounded disappointed. Acton thought back on the conversations that had taken place in front of the man, trying to figure out if he could possibly have known what they were truly searching for. He suppressed a frown, concluding the man might actually know, and in fact, probably did, Marius having mentioned the gold minutes ago.

Acton turned away, staring at the passing shantytown, his heart beating slightly faster.

Could we have just created a problem for Mr. Erasmus?

Lightman Residence

Fort Bragg, North Carolina

Sergeant Will "Spock" Lightman rubbed his eyes and yawned as he opened the front door. His eyebrow popped at the sight of his buddy, Sergeant Donald "Sweets" Peters.

"Dude, you need other friends or I need better ones. I told you about showing up here drunk in the middle of the night. I've got a family now."

Sweets pushed past him. "Yeah, yeah, that happened one time, and check your watch, it's not even dinner time."

"Huh?" Spock yawned again, glancing at the clock on the microwave.

Whadaya know!

He and his wife had been spending some quality time together, quality time that had ended in the bedroom, monkey business ensuing before much-deserved naps.

None of which explained why Sweets was here.

"Have we been called up?"

"No, but you did ignore my calls."

Spock shrugged. "Went to bed early." He grinned. "You know."

"Uh huh. Well, I just got a call from Red. Maggie's missing."

Spock's eyebrow nearly shot up to his hairline, a surge of adrenaline bringing everything into immediate focus. "Jesus, are you serious?"

"Yup. Apparently she's not at home, not at the office, and her cellphone's going straight to voicemail. The Colonel's the last to have seen her. She was apparently just getting ready to leave the office, but that was yesterday."

"And someone's checked it?"

"Yup, security swept the building. She's not there."

"Man, BD must be going apeshit."

"Yeah, he left on an op last night so it's up to us."

"Okay, give me a sec." He strode quickly to the bedroom, pulling on some clothes quietly, his still sleeping wife not deserving to be disturbed, not after how good she had made him feel earlier. He tiptoed out, firing her a text message with the gist of what was going on. Slipping his shoes on, he followed Sweets outside. "So what's BD want us to do?"

"Try and retrace her steps. See if she stopped anywhere after work, got stopped. Anything. He's worried something might have happened, you know, with her head wound."

Spock climbed into the passenger seat of Sweets' car. "Shit, never thought of that. Let's boogie." Sweets fired up the engine and they were quickly on their way to the Unit, a thought occurring to Spock. "Wait, she takes her car to work, right?"

"I think so."

"Did anybody think to check the parking lot?"

Sweets shrugged. "You'd think so, but I don't know for sure." He leaned over, letting one rip. "Oh God, I needed that."

Spock's eyes watered, his face scrunching up as he reached to lower the window. "For the love of God, what the hell was that?"

Sweets had a satisfied expression. "That, my friend, was the thunder from down under."

Spock waved a hand in front of his nose, leaning closer to the open window. "Dude, see a doctor. No healthy human being should make a smell like that."

"Your fault. You're the one who insisted on burritos yesterday." He let another one rip. "Oh man, can we stop by my place for a minute?"

Spock eyed him suspiciously. "Why?"

"I think I just shit myself."

"You're a pig."

"This surprises you?"

Spock grinned. "Not a bit." His eyes narrowed as he turned in his seat. "Ahh, did you really shit your pants, or were you just joking?"

Sweets leaned over, cocking a cheek. "Reach in and check for me."

Spock belted him in the shoulder.

"Ow, now I think I really did shit myself."

En route to Sabi Sabi Bush Lodge

Greater Kruger National Park, South Africa

"Recognize this?" Acton held up the small stone they had found carefully wrapped with the gold coins so Sipho could see it clearly without turning his head too far. Their guide took a quick glance and shrugged.

"Coal?"

"Yes."

"Sure, everyone knows what coal looks like." Sipho glanced in his mirror. "Why, you want more?"

Acton smiled, handing their clue to Laura who carefully rewrapped it. "Not exactly. Do you know if there are any old abandoned mines around here? And I mean *very* old, like over a hundred years."

Sipho's eyebrows climbed slightly, his eyes taking on a distant look as he thought for a moment. He flicked his lights on, it now dusk, Acton not realizing until that moment how dark it had become. Sipho glanced in the mirror. "Sorry, not that I can think of."

Acton frowned, yet wasn't willing to give up, not when they were so close. "No old cave entrances? Maybe boarded up?"

Sipho's eyes went wide. "Yes, actually, there is! In the preserve, I remember seeing such a thing once, years ago."

Acton and the others exchanged excited glances, Laura squeezing his hand. "Did you ever go inside?"

Sipho shook his head. "Nooo, you never know what could be living in there. Very unsafe. And no point. Tourists want to see animals outside, not hiding inside."

"Good point. Any chance you could take us there tomorrow?"

Sipho's head bobbed. "Sure, you're the boss, Mr. Professor. It's not that far from here. We could—wait, what's this?"

Somewhere up Shit's Creek

"Does anyone know where we are?"

Courtney Tasker ignored the question from Gina, instead kicking the tire of their Jag rental, the vehicle completely dead. Her boyfriend, Dyson, pulled out his cellphone, once again uselessly trying to get a signal, and once again uselessly telling everyone he didn't have one.

He's an idiot. Why am I dating him?

She jammed her hands onto her hips, an exasperated breath escaping, letting the world know how inconvenienced she was by this entire scenario.

A cat screeched in the distance.

A big one.

A chill raced up her spine, and for the first time, fear pushed annoyance aside.

Maybe this is why the guide said it wasn't safe.

Gina walked over, nervously scanning the area. "There's only one road, and we know it leads to the lodge. Maybe we should just start walking."

Gina's boyfriend shook his head. "It's going to be dark soon. And we're in Africa. There're animals here that could eat us!"

Gina glared at him. "So, what, Phil, you'd rather stay here and starve to death?"

Phil gave her a look. "We're hardly going to starve to death. There're not a lot of roads here, somebody is bound to come along and pick us up."

Courtney let out a growl, kicking the tire repeatedly. "Stupid! Stupid! Stupid! Stupid!" She yelped as she jammed her toe, hopping around for a moment. She screeched at the dead vehicle. "Stupid piece of shit!"

Phil winked at the others. "I guess you should have listened to the guide."

Courtney turned on him. "To hell with him, what does he know?"

"Umm, that this vehicle could break down in the middle of nowhere and leave us stranded to be eaten by lions?"

She jabbed a finger at him. "Watch your attitude! Remember who's paying for this trip!"

"How could I? You never let us forget that we're your charity cases."

Courtney glared at the ungrateful bastard. "I knew it was a mistake bringing you two. You just don't fit in, you're too…" She couldn't think of the word.

"What? Common? Middle-class?" Gina stepped toward her slightly. "I'll tell you one thing, I'd rather come from a family where my parents worked their asses off to put me in a good school, than one where everything was just handed to me."

Rage gripped Courtney as her so-called friends turned on her. "Go to hell! I can have your father fired in a heartbeat!"

Gina was having none of it. "That's the thing about you rich kids! You think you've got all this power, but you don't! Maybe your daddy can have mine fired, but *you* can't. You're just a spoiled rich bitch who thinks just because her family has money, she's better than everyone who doesn't."

Dyson finally decided to be a man, stepping between Courtney and her accoster. "Hey, you can't talk to my girlfriend that way!"

Gina glared at him. "Oh, but she can talk to me that way? Or those people back at the lodge? Or that poor woman who was just trying to feed her family?" She shook her head. "Have you listened to yourselves at all on this trip? You've talked down to everyone from the chauffeur in New York to that poor vendor. You haven't had a kind word to say to anyone in three days!"

Courtney flicked her wrist at her former friend. "You wouldn't understand, it's not your money paying for this trip. I expect excellent service for what this is costing me."

A burst of derision erupted from Gina's lips. "It's not *your* money either! It's your dad's. And just because his money bought him his job, doesn't make you any better than us!"

Courtney's fuse lit. It was one thing to attack her, but to attack her father was inexcusable. "He earned his job, he didn't buy it!"

"Riiight, a man who's never been involved in politics becomes the Secretary of the Treasury, not because he made a massive campaign donation, but because his résumé screamed experience."

Courtney's chest heaved in and out, the rage blinding. "You are *so* dead to me, you have no idea!"

Dyson pointed down the road, headlights bouncing toward them. "Somebody's coming!"

The argument was put on hold as they all stepped into the road, waving their arms as what turned out to be a safari vehicle came to a halt. Courtney pushed through the others. "Thank God you're here! Our car broke down."

A man stepped out from the rear and her heart sank as she recognized him.

"I guess you should have listened to my wife."

En route to Sabi Sabi Bush Lodge
Greater Kruger National Park, South Africa

No matter how much Acton would have loved to leave the four spoiled brats on the side of the road, this wasn't rural Maryland where you might be threatened by an aggressive squirrel after your nuts, this was Africa, where the wildlife was as likely to sniff you as eat you.

It did make for slightly cramped quarters, though only for the new arrivals. The vehicle was a good size, with two bench seats behind the driver designed to comfortably sit three across, there room for seven plus the guide—they were now nine crammed into the Toyota. Little Miss Priss, whom they had learned was named Courtney Tasker, was in the middle seats with her friends, Gorman having moved to the passenger seat beside Sipho, his wife now with them in the back. He could tell Courtney wasn't pleased to be jammed in with the others, there some conflict going on between them, glares exchanged. Courtney crammed against the door, attempting to avoid any physical contact with her boyfriend, the other couple sitting with their bodies turned away from her.

As long as they kept their mouths shut, he didn't care. If whatever dispute they were in the middle of were to break out again, he might just reconsider his decision, and leave them on the side of the road.

Sipho sensed the tension as well, heavier on the accelerator than before, the delay in getting the kids into the vehicle costing them precious minutes, the sun low on the horizon, the shadows long, a good distance still to cover.

Acton leaned back, his arm over Laura's shoulders, her head resting on his, and he closed his eyes, his head lolling to the side, the wind whipping in his face, his thoughts returning to the excitement of what tomorrow might bring. If Sipho did indeed know where the mine was, they might be about to solve a mystery over a century old, with nobody around to interfere, as so often happened.

He opened his eyes, noticing his head was stuck out the side of the vehicle, and for a moment he debated sticking his tongue out to the side and see what all the rage was in the canine community, but something caught his eye. He turned back and frowned, several sets of headlights behind them.

"We've got company."

Sipho glanced in the mirror as everyone turned to look, and Acton felt the vehicle surge slightly faster.

"Hotel guests?" suggested Laura.

It was a possibility, though Acton felt a pit form in his stomach. "Could be, but they're coming awfully fast."

A sound Acton recognized too well shattered the peace as he pushed Laura forward. "Everyone down!"

The girls in the middle seats screamed, the brat's boyfriend popping up in his seat as he spun around like an idiot. "Was that a gunshot?"

Acton reached forward, punching him in the stomach, causing him to double over, dropping the vacant target that was his head. "Yes. Now stay the hell down!"

Gunfire continued and Sipho pushed harder on the accelerator, but their situation appeared hopeless. As Acton peered over the rear of his seat, he could see the others were gaining, this safari vehicle not designed for speed, especially on these roads. He could feel the backend fishtail, Sipho easing off the accelerator, seeking a speed that would allow him to maintain control.

And to top it all off, as this was a safari vehicle, it was completely open to the elements.

And bullets.

It was a deathtrap, overflowing with human flesh.

He looked to the front and saw Gorman had managed to wedge a good chunk of his body under the dash, as protected as he could be. The four morons in the center seat seemed to be having problems, the two couples continuing their feud, refusing to touch each other. He reached forward and grabbed the one he had punched. "I don't know what the hell is going on with you idiots, but put it aside for now, or you're going to die! Girls, lie on the floor, I don't care if you hate each other right now. And boys, start to act like men, and protect your women. Cover them with your bodies, or so help me God, I'm going to toss all of you out of here in the next sixty seconds!"

They all froze, staring at him for a moment, clearly debating whether he was serious.

"Now!"

Courtney dove to the floor first, rolling to her side as her frenemy lay beside her, the two boyfriends bending over, trying to cover them, all their bodies at least now below the seatback.

Acton lay across the back seat, Angeline already lying on the floor, Laura over her, allowing him to use most of the seat so he could occasionally assess their increasingly deteriorating situation.

He glanced forward, making eye contact with Sipho in the rearview mirror. "Who are they?"

Sipho's face was racked with guilt, that much was obvious, yet he said nothing.

"Sipho, who the hell are they?"

Sipho glanced at him briefly, his hands gripping the steering wheel as he fought to maintain control. "I-I think it might be my brother, Tladi."

Acton felt his chest tighten. "Why? What makes you say that?"

"I-I think he may be after whatever you found."

"But we found nothing!"

"He-he doesn't know that. He just knows rich white people were excited about a medallion. Everyone around here knows about the gold. Maybe he thinks you found it."

Laura poked her head up slightly. "But why would he shoot at his own brother?"

Shame replaced the guilt. "My brother is a bad man. He's a poacher."

Acton exchanged a look with Laura, recognizing her anger at this revelation. They both hated criminals with a passion. He personally felt that those who committed acts of vandalism should simply be shot, there no purpose to their criminal acts. Thieves at least had a purpose, feeding some sort of need, though he felt they should be shot as well. Why should someone be allowed to live who felt they were entitled to the things you worked hard to accumulate in your life?

But poachers? They were something else entirely. Not only were they motivated by greed, they were destroying species and ecosystems, risking the extinction of creatures that had survived successfully long before man had come along, and certainly longer than some cultures had decided certain parts of their anatomy could be enhanced through the senseless slaughter of innocent wildlife.

Poachers had a special corner of Hell reserved, just for them.

But unfortunately for him and his friends, these particular ones hadn't been sent there yet.

Sipho glanced back as more shots rang out. "Should we stop?"

Acton shook his head. "No." At this moment, he wasn't sure if he trusted Sipho, the promise of millions in gold almost irresistible anywhere in the world, the allure to someone who lived in near abject poverty perhaps enough to turn even the purest of souls.

More shots, Acton noting for the first time they hadn't been hit yet.

Warning shots, or poorly aimed shots?

"What should we do?" asked Gorman from the front seat.

Sipho pressed harder on the accelerator, answering the question for them, and returning Acton's faith in this man they barely knew. "We need to get to the lodge."

He suddenly remembered something, reaching down and shaking Laura's shoulder. "Get your satphone out!"

She reached into her pocket, retrieving their lifeline to the outside world. "Who am I going to call? It's not like I've got a phonebook here."

He peered at the lead vehicle, now only a few hundred yards from their bumper. "Call Hugh, he'll be able to contact the authorities."

Laura's eyes widened at the suggestion, rapidly dialing. Courtney shoved her head up once again, pushing her boyfriend aside as he tried to force her back to the floor. "Tell him I'm Courtney Tasker! I'm the daughter of the Treasury Secretary. My daddy will find a way to help us!"

Acton's eyebrows rose slightly at the revelation as he peered out the back. "How much farther?"

"Too far! Another forty minutes at least!" cried Sipho with a glance over his shoulder.

It was hopeless. At these speeds, they were liable to go off the road, especially in the growing darkness, and besides, the other vehicles were still gaining.

"Maybe we should just surrender?"

Acton frowned at Laura's suggestion, shaking his head as she dialed again. "We can't risk it, and besides, I don't think they're shooting at us."

"What makes you think that?"

"We haven't been hit." He spotted the rifle lying between the seats, next to Sipho. He reached over and grabbed it, checking to see if it was loaded. He turned around, took aim, then fired, a headlight blown out, the hood flipping up on the lead vehicle.

"Good shot!"

"Lucky shot. Ammo?" Acton turned around, Sipho gesturing to the glove compartment, Gorman retrieving several boxes of ammo and handing them back to Acton. He quickly opened a box, shoving the contents into his pocket.

"What the hell do they want?" cried Courtney from her hiding place, the terror in her voice making her seem more human.

He fired again, missing, Laura grabbing him by the leg to get his attention. She pointed at the satphone. "I've got Hugh!"

"Please help us!" cried Courtney, her boyfriend wisely shoving her back down.

There might be hope for that boy yet.

Acton reloaded as Laura spoke to the one friend who might be able to help, more shots firing, this time sounding like they were getting closer. It was inevitable, they were going to be stopped, and any desperate call for help now was for a rescue hours or days away.

He took aim, wondering if pissing them off was a wise move.

Probably not.

He fired again.

Hugh Reading Residence

Whitehall, London, England

Interpol Agent Hugh Reading inhaled deeply, the curry that had just arrived from Indian Express filling his nostrils, the scent of his favorite dish—chicken tikka masala with pilau rice and a side of naan—overwhelming his senses. He sighed, taking a sip of his pint of John Smith's Extra Smooth.

This is the life.

He frowned.

Too bad you don't have anyone to share it with.

His son was coming over tomorrow for dinner, something he looked forward to. He hoped he might convince him to go to the pub for a pint, something they had yet to do together. It was only recently that they had reestablished regular contact, the boy holding a grudge for more than a decade over the divorce.

It hadn't mattered to him that the separation had been mutual and fairly friendly, all things considered. And it had definitely been for the best. Marriage and his job as a detective were not compatible, at least not for a detective with ambition. His job had cost him his family, though it would have happened regardless of what he was doing, he and his wife young lovers that grew apart as they became adults.

But now, now that he had been forced to step aside, to leave the job he had loved with Scotland Yard, he had more time on his hands, and an olive branch had been extended to his son.

And accepted.

I wonder what we'll have tomorrow.

There was no way he was cooking, any effort likely to scare the poor lad off for good. He dipped his head toward his plate, deeply inhaling once more.

We could do this again.

He shoved his fork into the dish, lifting a steaming helping of the rice toward his mouth, his eyes closing in anticipation.

His phone vibrated on the table beside him.

Bloody hell.

He stared at it for a moment then swallowed the bite, savoring every chew as the explosion of flavors conquered his taste buds, refusing to let the unknown number interfere with his enjoyment of this moment.

The first bite of a meal anticipated.

He moaned with pleasure.

India might have invented it, but we perfected it.

The phone stopped vibrating, then resumed moments later.

He sighed heavily, putting his fork down and swiping his thumb over the display.

"Hello?"

"Hugh?"

He recognized Laura Palmer's voice and smiled. "Oh, hello Laura, you caught me in the mid—"

"Hugh! You've got to help us!"

His chest tightened and he shoved his food away, grabbing a notepad and pen sitting on the nearby counter, the fear in his friend's voice obvious. "Go ahead."

"We're in South Africa. We're on the road leading to the Sabi Sabi Bush Lodge in Kruger National Park. We're being pursued by poachers who think we've found the Kruger Gold. They're shooting at us and there's no way we're going to reach help in time."

A young woman shouted something unintelligible as he jotted notes.

"Listen, we picked up four strays. One of them says she's the daughter of the Treasury Secretary for the United States. You need to get us help."

The distinct sound of gunfire filled his ear.

Gunfire that sounded close.

"Are you okay?"

"James is returning fire, but there're three vehicles after us and we've only got one rifle."

Another voice shouted in the background. "Look out!"

"James!"

There was a loud series of sounds, as if the phone had been dropped, then silence.

"Laura!"

Road to Sabi Sabi Bush Lodge

Greater Kruger National Park, South Africa

Tladi stepped from the truck before it came to a complete halt, rushing toward the overturned Toyota. Rage filled his heart at the fact his own brother had fired on them, though he had a suspicion it was the rich white people who were doing the actual shooting. He motioned for his men to surround the vehicle, they complying, training their weapons on the moaning passengers as he searched for his brother in the wreckage.

His jaw dropped when he finally spotted him, still in his seat, there no signs of movement.

"Sipho!" He repeatedly kicked at the windshield, ramming it with the heel of his boot before it finally gave way. He reached in, hauling out the glass and tossing it onto the side of the road. Dropping to his knees, he put a hand on his brother's face. "Sipho, are you okay?"

There was no response. He grabbed the moaning man whose body lay overtop his brother, hauling him through the windshield, two of his men rushing forward to help, the man heavy.

"Please, my wife!"

Tladi ignored the man's pleas, as did his men. "Brother, speak to me!" He shook Sipho's shoulder. He moaned. Tladi's heart leaped in relief as he let out a sigh and a silent prayer. "Thank God you're okay." His brother's eyes fluttered open.

"Brother!" he gasped.

"Yes, it's me." Tladi felt a flash of anger wash through him. "Why did you run? You knew who it was!"

The only response was a moan.

I have to get him out of there.

He reached in and pulled his eldest brother from the seat and through the windshield. Sipho cried out in agony, but Tladi continued, committed to removing him from the overturned vehicle. He laid his brother on the ground then gasped at the large gash in the side of Sipho's stomach, cut by something, probably a large rock on the ground as the vehicle skidded on its side.

Blood was everywhere, a long trail of it stretching the entire distance he had pulled his brother, his clothes soaked with the precious fluid. Tladi slapped both hands on the wound, turning to his men. "Get me something to stop the bleeding."

They stood there, staring.

"Now!"

One of his men, Jacob, shrugged. "We don't have anything, boss."

Sipho reached up and grabbed Tladi by the back of the neck, pulling him closer. "Y-you're better than this."

Sipho collapsed, exhausted, and Tladi watched in horror as all life drained from his brother's face, his eyes dead, his life over. A pit formed in Tladi's stomach as he clasped his brother's lifeless hand still around his neck. He placed it gently on his brother's chest then climbed to his feet, rage returning, sorrow and any sense of responsibility forgotten.

He turned to the nearest captive, all the tourists now lined up, all unscathed, unlike his brother. He aimed his weapon at an arrogant looking young white man, someone too young to have earned his way here, clearly from a wealthy family.

A wealthy family that was about to pay.

"My brother is dead."

The man held up his hands, shaking his head. "Hey, dude, I had nothing to do—"

Tladi fired, silencing the privileged scum, the boy dropping in a heap, the girl he had been standing with screaming then bolting into the dark. His men turned to give chase when he raised a hand. "Let her go. She'll be dead by morning." He turned to the older people, including two black South Africans who had forgotten where they came from. "Besides, we don't need her. They're who we want."

Road to Sabi Sabi Bush Lodge
Greater Kruger National Park, South Africa

Laura rushed to the young man's side as everyone else stood stunned. This wasn't her first time in a situation like this, dominated by death and violence, and she had little doubt it wouldn't be her last. She dropped to her knees, checking the boy for a pulse, finding none.

She glared at the man who had shot him. "You didn't need to do that."

He sneered at her. "My brother died, so one of you dies. Eye for an eye."

Laura rose, pointing at Sipho. "Your brother died because of *you*, not because of this boy."

The other young woman cried out, sobbing uncontrollably, her boyfriend holding her, desperately trying to silence her, Laura certain he was afraid any undue attention might result in their own deaths.

"Watch your mouth, or you're next."

Laura glared at Sipho's brother but bit her tongue. Clearly, life meant little to this piece of garbage, and with the guilt and grief of killing his own brother, he would be unpredictable.

A gun was shoved in her face.

"Get back with the others."

She stepped back slowly toward Gorman who held his shaking wife, Laura's eyes searching the near darkness for any sign of James, his ejection from the vehicle something these men didn't appear to be aware of.

And just as they had no idea he existed, she had no idea if he were alive.

Her heart slammed as she thought of the myriad possibilities, her mind dwelling on the most awful. The fall could have killed him, or worse, left him injured, only to face some horrible fate at the jaws of the unforgiving nature that surrounded them.

Please, God, let him be okay.

He had to be.

For some reason, she knew he was alive, convinced if he weren't she'd sense it, their love so deep.

Those aren't the thoughts of a scientist.

And they weren't. They were the thoughts of a desperate soul, barely clinging to control.

She looked at the murderer. "Sipho said your name was Tladi."

"Yes."

"What is it you want?"

He smiled, stepping toward her, weapon still raised. "I want the gold, miss, the gold."

Footsteps rapidly approached, accompanied by panicked breathing. Acton jumped up, grabbing the girl, slapping a hand over her mouth before she could scream and reveal their position.

"It's okay, it's me. Just keep quiet."

She twisted her head, staring at him with wild eyes, the light from the moon revealing her terror, and her identity. He had to admit he was disappointed it was the hateful girl who had managed to escape, there others more deserving.

He stared her in the eyes. "Are you going to keep quiet?"

She nodded.

He slowly removed his hand.

"They killed him!"

He slapped his hand over her mouth again, glaring at her. "They'll kill both of us if you don't keep your voice down. Now, are you going to keep quiet? Last chance."

She nodded again, and this time, as he removed his hand, kept her mouth shut.

A good thing, since the only other option he could think of was a sleeper hold.

"How many are there?"

She shook her head. "I-I don't know. At least ten, maybe more."

"Who did they kill?"

"Dyson. My boyfriend."

Acton frowned. He was a punk, though so were most early-twenties boys trying to be men. "Why?"

"I think because the driver died."

Acton cursed. Sipho was a good man, a man he could see as a friend if there had been enough time, but now he was dead. All because of greed. And if it was his brother that had attacked them, he'd be feeling guilty over Sipho's death.

And that made him unpredictable.

"Did they say anything else?"

Another headshake. "No, I-I just ran."

"Okay, I need to get closer to hear what's going on."

"Closer!" She slapped two hands over her own mouth before removing them slowly. "Closer?" she whispered. "Are you insane?"

"Certifiable, but that's my wife out there, and I'm going to save her, even if I have to kill every single one of those bastards. And in order to do that, I need intel." He looked at her, shaking like the grass around her. "You stay here. I'll come back for you. If something happens to me, wait until they leave, then keep going down this road until you get to the lodge."

"B-but what about animals?"

He handed her the gun, never having lost his grip on it despite his fall. "Do you know how to use this?"

"I've done some skeet shooting with my daddy."

He emptied his pockets of the remaining ammo, handing it to her. "If anything gets close, be big, be loud, and if that doesn't work, then blast this at it. It should scare pretty much anything away."

"A-are you going to save my friends?"

He looked at her. "I'm going to try and save everyone. Now wait here, and try not to shoot me when I come back."

"Umm, shouldn't we have a code word or something, you know, like in the movies?"

Acton smiled slightly, it a good idea. And he decided it would be best if the panicking young woman chose it. "Any suggestions?"

"Umm, how about Talia and Deavon?"

Acton's eyes narrowed. "Who are they?"

"Lil' Bratz dolls."

Oy!

"Fine. I'll be back as soon as I can, but don't be alarmed if it takes a while. I might not be able to move very quickly. Just keep your head down and keep quiet until I get back or they leave."

"Okay."

He turned to leave when she reached out and grabbed his arm.

"I-I'm sorry for the way I acted."

He looked into her eyes, eyes that darted away with embarrassment and shame, then met his with an earnestness that had him believing her. He patted her hand. "We were all young once. Don't worry about it."

She lunged forward, dropping the gun and wrapping her arms around him, her shoulders heaving. "Be careful," she gasped.

"I will." He patted her back and gently pushed her away, turning and rapidly moving through the tall grass before she could delay him any further. He had to hear what they were planning.

Laura's life might just depend on it.

"Where's the gold?"

Laura glared at Tladi. "I have no idea what you're talking about."

Tladi pointed at the others. "Perhaps if I kill some more of your friends, you might be more willing to talk."

Laura decided their best chance of survival was to make him think they truly did know nothing for now, the longer she could delay their leaving this location, the more chance Reading would have to get the local authorities here. "You can kill everyone, it won't change the fact I don't know what you're talking about. If you let us go now, nothing will happen to you. We don't know who you are, so there's nothing we can tell the authorities."

Tladi smiled slightly, pointing his weapon at Sipho. "That was my brother, and you know that. If I let you go, you will tell them this, and they will find me." He wagged the gun at her. "You think I'm stupid, don't you? A dumb kaffir that you can outwit?"

Laura tensed, it clear there would be no tricking this man. She had been hoping for an idiot, not because of the color of his skin, but because he was a criminal.

No such luck.

And these men would kill them all to save themselves unless they had some reason to keep them alive. And right now, she could think of only two reasons to do so—information that might lead them to the gold, or the far more terrifying reason, the satisfaction of the carnal lust in the eyes of the men around her, three women here they might have their way with before ultimately killing them.

She had to protect herself and the others from that fate, and there was only one way she could think of.

Leverage the little bit of knowledge they had.

She stared at him. "Why do you think we've got the gold?"

He reached forward, ripping the medallion off her chest. He held up the imprint of the Kruger coin. "Because of this. I know the old man found it in the field."

Laura's mouth went dry, there no way he should be privy to that information, unless—the thought turned her stomach. "H-how do you know that?"

"Because Florence told me."

Laura's chest tightened with trepidation and rage. She glared at him, her fists clenching. "What did you do to her?"

Tladi chuckled, exchanging a glance with his men. "Nothing that hasn't been done before."

"You bastard! She's just a girl!"

His hand darted out, grabbing her between the legs. "And you're a woman. Maybe I should show you what I did. It made her talk, maybe it will make you."

"Just tell him, for God's sake!"

Laura glanced at Angeline, her eyes wide with terror, her husband patting her head as he held her tight.

Tladi smiled, the fact there was a secret now revealed. "Yes, why don't you tell me, for *God's* sake?" He tapped the barrel of his gun against her chest. "And your own."

Acton slithered through the tall grass until within earshot, not hearing much beyond demands to know where the gold was. Laura was taking the brunt of the questioning, the others saying nothing beyond a plea from Angeline to reveal the secret.

"Fine, I'll tell you."

Good girl, buy time.

"But I want you to let them go."

There was a laugh, probably from Tladi, Acton crawling closer to see. He frowned at the sight, Tladi standing in front of Laura, his weapon pointed at her chest. "You're in no position to bargain." He cocked his head toward the others, huddled together near the rear of the overturned vehicle. "How about I let them live? Does that sound like a fair deal?"

Laura said nothing, her jaw squared as he knew she was evaluating her options.

Tladi pushed his gun into one of her breasts.

Bastard!

"Speak, or die."

She sighed. "It's in an old mine."

Tladi smiled, removing the weapon from Laura's chest. "That's better. Where?"

Laura pointed at the body of Sipho. "Ask him."

The gun shoved into Laura's stomach and she doubled over with a gasp. Every muscle in Acton's body tensed as he prepared to spring from the darkness, but he resisted the urge to tear the bastard's throat out.

"Don't get smart with me. What mine?"

Laura shrugged. "I don't know. Sipho said he knew where it was."

One of Tladi's men stepped out of the shadows, glancing about nervously. "Boss, we gotta go before someone comes."

Tladi peered down the road in both directions then up at the sky. "Okay, let's move out. We'll get the answers from her at the camp." Tladi grabbed Laura by the arm, dragging her to one of their vehicles still idling nearby. Acton sat up slightly, trying to keep her in sight, desperate to call out to her, to let her know he was alive, that there was still hope.

But he couldn't reveal his position.

He smiled.

Then executed a birdcall he had perfected in Peru, a fairly decent impression of a little blue heron, something not native to this area.

Laura's head jerked in his direction for an instance before she feigned a neck spasm, his location secure.

She had received his message.

He was alive.

Now it was up to her to stay the same.

The Unit

Fort Bragg, North Carolina

"That's Maggie's car, isn't it?"

Sweets looked to where Spock pointed then frowned. "Yeah, that's definitely hers." He cursed. "That means she never left."

Spock agreed. "Or left with someone else."

Sweets pulled into a vacant spot. "Or was abducted from here."

Spock climbed out, his eyes on her car. "I think that's probably a stretch. This is Bragg. It should be secure."

Sweets closed his door, locking the car with his fob. "I wouldn't be so sure of that, but you'd think someone would have seen something, at least. It's fairly busy around here."

Spock shook his head as they walked over to her vehicle. "Late on a Friday night? Not necessarily." He peered through the passenger side window, Sweets doing the same on the other side. "I don't see a purse or anything."

"Me neither."

Spock pulled out his phone, taking shots of the interior then a few of the exterior. "I'm sending these to BD, see if he notices anything odd." He sighed. "Man, he's going to freak."

Sweets nodded. "Yup, *this* is why I'm staying single."

Spock's eyebrow popped as the photos transmitted. "Riiight, *this* is why."

Sweets gave him a look. "What are you trying to say?"

"I'm saying you're undateable. Every relationship you've had has been whirlwind—fall for them hard, get too serious too quick."

Sweets held a hand over his heart. "Ouch. And what's wrong with that?"

"I don't know. Why not ask all the women who've broken up with you? They oughta be able to give you some insight." Sweets opened his mouth to defend himself when Spock spotted Red arriving, cutting him off with a raised finger. "Hold that thought." He strode across the parking lot toward Red, Sweets following, muttering in protest as Red exited his vehicle.

"Is that Maggie's car?"

"Yup," replied Spock.

"Shit, something's definitely wrong." Red turned and limped quickly toward the Delta HQ, impatiently clearing security. "Is the Colonel here?"

"Not yet, Sergeant," replied the corporal manning the front desk. "He's fifteen minutes out."

"I need access to his office immediately."

"Sorry, Sergeant, I can't allow that."

Spock's eyebrow rose at the balls the unfortunate corporal was displaying, following the book as he had been trained.

Red jabbed a finger at him. "Do *you* have access, Corporal?"

"Sergeant?"

"*Someone* needs to look in his office. Maggie Harris may be inside, injured."

"Ahh, Sergeant, I haven't—"

Red's hands balled into fists. "Corporal, either you open that door, or I'm kicking it down!"

The poor corporal appeared confused, and Spock had to feel for the young man, doing his job properly, flexibility to adapt to the situation at hand drummed out of soldiers at that age and rank. He was probably terrified of what the Colonel might do to him if he found out he allowed a lowly sergeant to access his office without permission.

And that meant this young corporal didn't know the Colonel.

Red stormed past the corporal, limping toward Colonel Clancy's office at the end of the hall, Spock and Sweets on his heels, the corporal rushing after them.

"Sergeant! I can't allow you to do this!"

Spock turned, cutting him off, placing a finger on the corporal's chest. "Then don't make him do it. I *guarantee* you, the Colonel will want this door opened, regardless of what we find."

The corporal tried to move around him though seemed reluctant to push Spock out of the way as Red and Sweets continued down the hall. Finally, he grabbed his radio. "I'm calling it in!"

Spock smiled. "You do that. Then call maintenance."

The corporal's eyes narrowed. "Why?"

"Because there's going to be a door to fix."

Road to Sabi Sabi Bush Lodge

Greater Kruger National Park, South Africa

Acton watched helplessly as they pulled away, the small convoy leaving the road and heading northeast, away from the lodge and away from civilization. He was under no illusions of keeping up with them on foot, though he might be able to track them, all the vehicles equipped with large tires with thick, knobby treads. If he remembered his forecast, there was no rain in it, so any trail they left should still be there by morning.

For now, he just had to track them while Reading worked to get help into the area.

And there was no time to waste. He turned toward where Courtney should be hiding. "You can come out now!" He could hear her pushing through the grass toward him as he searched the overturned vehicle for supplies. He grabbed all the water and ammo he could find, a hunting knife off of Sipho's belt, and an emergency kit stashed in the back, a quick inventory revealing some rations, a flashlight, a tent, sleeping bags, and a first aid kit.

Everything they should need to survive the night, though little to help them engage a dozen hostiles.

"How far is it to the lodge?" asked Courtney as she emerged from the grass.

He pointed down the road. "A couple of hours, I'd guess. Just keep walking that way and you'll get there eventually."

Courtney stared at him. "Aren't you coming?"

He shook his head. "No, I'm going after them."

"Are you nuts! They'll kill you!"

Acton shoved all his scavenged supplies into a backpack that Gorman had been carrying, emptying out the man's spare clothes, discovering a few chocolate bars tucked into the bottom.

So the belly's from not being on dig sites, huh?

"You go back to the lodge and tell them what happened. Have them send help."

Courtney shook her head. "I'll be eaten by something before I get there."

Acton pointed at the rifle in her hand. "Use that like I told you."

She shook her head, vehemently. "No, we need to stick together."

"You'll just slow me down."

She gave him a look. "I'm half your age. If anyone's slowing anyone down, it's you."

Ouch!

The sad thing was she was probably right, though youth and stamina were one thing, experience another.

"She told them they were looking for the mine. If one of those guys knows where it is, they'll head directly there, and once they find the gold, they'll kill all the witnesses. I don't have time to debate this."

"There's actually gold?"

"Possibly. It doesn't matter if there is or not, *they* think there is, and if they find it, or don't find it, when they've decided my wife and the others aren't worth anything, then they'll kill them."

Courtney's hand darted to her chest. "You think so?"

He nodded toward the body of her boyfriend. "Ask him." He slung the backpack over his shoulder, shrugging his other arm into the second strap, adjusting it so it would be snug to cut down on chafing.

He tested the flashlight he had found in the emergency kit then aimed it toward the lodge. "That way. Now."

"No way. I'm sticking with you."

Acton suppressed the growl of frustration desperate to escape. "Fine." He pointed to the horizon where the lights from the vehicles were still visible. "We need to get there as quickly as possible."

Courtney held out a hand, presenting the vast distance as if it were his to enjoy. "Don't let me stop you."

He turned, breaking out into a jog with a frown on his face.

This isn't going to work.

En Route to Heathrow Airport, London, England

Reading gripped the Oh Jesus! bar as the cabby followed his instructions, careening through traffic under the authority of an Interpol agent who had no authority. His flight left in less than an hour, and he couldn't risk missing it, his friends in trouble. A quick call to Arthur Pleasance, someone he had worked with at Heathrow when he first investigated Acton for murder, secured a promise to smooth his way through security.

Though he had to get there first.

His desperate hope was that by the time he reached South Africa, all would be resolved, but he'd never be able to live with himself if he were to stay behind and let others, others who lacked the vested interest he had in the situation, deal with it at their leisure.

The wheels, however, were in motion. The moment his call had been cut off with Laura, he had called Interpol, his Director making certain the South African authorities were notified, as well as the Americans.

And he had been ordered to remain put—it was not his job.

He had respectfully told his boss to sod off and that he was on vacation for a week effective immediately.

He had then done something he hated doing—purchased a last minute ticket using an account Laura had given him access to for emergencies.

To say Laura was rich was an understatement. To say she was generous was equally so. He cringed at using her account for this, though she'd never object, and in fact would likely insist upon it, if she were reachable.

And she wasn't.

Whatever had happened in those final seconds had taken the phone offline.

Permanently.

That, unfortunately, meant there was nothing for them to trace. But she had given a rough location, and hopefully the locals would get their act together with boots on the ground without delay. Yet that all assumed these poachers hadn't already relocated them, and with the speed at which things moved in Africa, he had no doubt it would be hours before any local authorities reached the site.

He checked his watch.

Bloody hell. They'll be dead by then.

He pulled out his phone, sending a message to a number he was one of a privileged few to have.

Desperate times.

He watched the buildings whip by as he searched for another way to help, a smile suddenly appearing.

Leather!

University College London Dig Site
Lower Nubia, Egypt

Lt. Colonel Cameron Leather, retired, sat in his tent, frowning. His employer was on holiday, which was nothing out of the ordinary, and that fact had zero effect on his day-to-day responsibilities. His job, and that of his men, was to protect the various dig sites Laura Palmer and her husband had. At the moment, that included Acton's dig in Peru and hers here in Egypt.

He pulled his shirt from his chest, it stuck to him like a sweaty lover. The heat was unbearable at times, this after all the middle of the desert, but you got used to it. He had just returned from Peru, where it was a hell of a lot cooler than here, so had yet to acclimate. Out of fairness, he rotated his teams between the two sites and completely out of the cycle, the company he had founded after retiring from the British Special Air Services, having contracts with other clients.

But Laura Palmer's money bought *his* services.

And they had definitely been needed over the past few years.

He had been hired through government referrals and had expected a routine assignment. Never had he expected to be battling Islamic extremists in this very location, Chinese in the Amazon, or ancient cults in Iceland.

It was a great gig.

He had feared retirement would be boring, though as long as he worked for Laura Palmer, he doubted it ever would be, which was just fine by him, though the price had been high, too many of his men dead.

But that was the job, and they had died protecting the students that he could hear on the other side of the thin tent, two of whom stood in front of him right now.

Their teacher was on vacation, and their teacher, as was her too often exercised prerogative, had left with no security detail. He had to admire that. She refused to live her life in fear, despite everything that had happened to her and her husband. And with the Triarii hopefully out of their lives, things might be less complicated from now on, though those two put together seemed to invite trouble.

It kept life interesting.

And a safari in South Africa should be no concern, though apparently she had missed her normal check-in with her grad student, Terrence Mitchell.

It was this lack of communication that was the subject of the earnest conversation with Mitchell and his wife.

Earnestness that needed to be calmed.

"She could have just forgotten. I wouldn't worry about it."

Mitchell nodded, apparently unconvinced. "Possibly. I just thought you should know I hadn't heard from her. I tried her satphone myself, and it's not working."

This caught Leather's attention, his eyes narrowing.

Mitchell sensed he might not have lost the argument. "I mean, she's not answering, it just goes straight to voicemail."

Leather relaxed slightly. "Again, nothing out of the ordinary. They could be on an overnighter in the middle of nowhere and the battery went dead. Nothing to panic about yet."

Mitchell sighed. "Yeah, I guess you're right, but bloody hell, ever since she met him there's been nothing but trouble!"

Leather chuckled, a hint of jealousy still there, the young lad once having a fairly obvious crush on his professor. He had done well, though, marrying the pretty young thing that stood beside him.

Jenny elbowed her husband. "Some would say ever since *he* met *her*, *his* life has been hell."

Mitchell grunted. "Some would, but they'd be wrong."

Leather's satphone rang and he grabbed it, answering the call. "Leather."

"Hi Cameron, Hugh Reading. We've got a problem."

Lee Fang Residence

Philadelphia, Pennsylvania

Dylan Kane moaned in ecstasy as the strong hands of the Asian goddess straddling his back worked their magic. It had been a tough couple of weeks extracting himself from China after the events in South Korea, the borders tightened up while tensions were allowed to ease. He had been forced to hole up at his friend Chan Chao's place for a few days before a freighter transport was arranged, unfortunately taking him to Singapore rather than the closer Japan.

But no matter. He had survived, returned home for a far too infrequent visit with the love of his life, Lee Fang, who was working away the remnants of the hell his body had endured over days spent in a metal box.

And it *was* hell.

He wasn't ashamed to admit that when his contact in Singapore had cracked open the special delivery, his friend had run from the smell, turning a hose on him for ten minutes after ordering him to strip in the backyard.

And it was one of the more refreshing showers he could remember.

Life as a Special Agent in the CIA wasn't easy, and was usually lonely, a flurry of one night stands and meaningless affairs seeming fun on the big screen, though torture to the heart in real life. He had always planned on being dead by forty, there no point in a long-term relationship, but then he had met Fang, a fellow intelligence operative, exiled from her home, as alone as he was, a stranger in a strange land.

He rolled over, smiling up at her. "I love you."

She beamed, dropping on top of him, kissing him deeply. "I love you too."

A warmth spread through him, a feeling he would never tire of, a feeling he had never experienced until he had met her, and a feeling he knew, if it were ever lost, might never be found again.

"I missed you."

He smiled. "I could tell by the way you mauled me when I came through the door."

She giggled, swirling a finger around one of his nipples. "You surprised me. I didn't know you'd be back so soon."

"Well, you know the job. It doesn't exactly let me post my schedule online."

She shrugged. "I understand. It makes it more exciting."

An electric pulse surged through his wrist, his watch secretly indicating he had an important message.

"Ugh."

Her eyes narrowed. "What?"

He shook the wrist with the CIA issued device.

Fang frowned, sitting up. "But you just got here!" She gyrated her hips, drawing in a deep, slow breath as she closed her eyes. "You check your messages. I'll be a moment."

Kane laughed as he entered a coded sequence of button presses around the dial, a message projected on the back of the crystal indicating he had a secure communication on his private service. Years ago, he had set up a clandestine way of communicating with trusted contacts without the CIA's knowledge, a safety net in case someone, somewhere, decided he was expendable—and he didn't agree with their assessment.

Fang moaned louder, Kane leaning back and groaning as he reached over and grabbed his laptop, flipping it open as the most spectacular sight he could imagine continued to take care of her own business—he was merely a tool in the equation.

He pressed his thumb against the biometric sensor then launched his secure communications service. He frowned at the message from the British Interpol agent, Hugh Reading, a message that could mean only one thing.

The professor was in trouble.

What the hell is it with him?

Fang cried out, her fingers tearing at his chest like a lioness as he turned his attention back to her for a moment, doing his part to make her feel as good as she made him, it not taking long for him to join her in shared ecstasy before she collapsed atop him once again, her chest heaving, her breath hot on his neck.

"Oh, God, I love it when you're home."

He kissed her. "Evidently."

She gave him a peck then rolled off, a puddle of satisfied flesh content to let him finish whatever had distracted him. "Langley?"

"No, Hugh Reading."

She propped herself up on one elbow, her eyes narrowed. "Really? The professors?"

Kane dialed his phone. "We're about to find out."

Outside Colonel Clancy's Office, The Unit

Fort Bragg, North Carolina

Red was about to kick open the outer door to Colonel Clancy's office when Spock held up a hand.

"Wait, you wanna sprain the other ankle?"

Red stepped aside, presenting the door with an outstretched hand to the healthier warrior. "Be my guest."

Spock smiled at him. "Thank you." Then planted a swift kick next to the lock, the door splintering. Slamming it with his shoulder, the door flew open, Spock stumbling inside, Red and Sweets following.

At first glance, Red saw nothing out of the ordinary. "I'll check her computer." He rounded her desk as Spock flicked the light switch.

Red gasped.

Maggie lay on the floor behind the desk, blood trickling from her nose, a small pool on the carpet. He rushed to her side, pointing at Spock. "Ambulance, now!"

Spock grabbed the desk phone so there'd be no doubt of the location, as Sweets seized the corner of the desk, swinging it out of the way.

Red leaned close to Maggie's ear. "Maggie, can you hear me?"

A weak moan, little else.

"Everything's going to be okay. We're here now."

"BD?"

He could barely hear her, Spock stepping into the hallway with the distraught corporal, the young man now realizing his folly. "He's on an op. I'll let him know we found you."

Her eyes fluttered open and she stared at him. "No, he'll j-just worry." Her voice was barely a whisper, the words mumbled, difficult to understand, and judging from her face, Red had a suspicion of what had happened.

And could only pray he was wrong.

Virgin Atlantic Flight 601

Heathrow Airport, London, England

Reading sank into the plush leather of first class, suddenly realizing why the ticket was so damned expensive, the opulence surrounding him something he had never experienced before on a long-haul flight, unless blessed to be in Laura's private jet.

And it made him feel guilty.

Bloody hell, this isn't right.

He turned in his seat, looking at the poor bastards in economy, and noted it was completely full, making him feel better that he hadn't made a mistake and missed a cheaper seat.

He sighed.

Laura won't mind. This is like me buying her a coffee.

He grunted.

A fancy one, but a coffee nonetheless.

His phone vibrated and he checked the display.

Blocked.

He swiped his thumb, putting the phone to his ear. "Reading."

"Hey Hugh, it's Dylan. Everything okay?"

Reading snorted. "With Jim and Laura in our lives, is it ever?"

Kane chuckled. "What now?"

"I just got a call from Laura. They're in South Africa, near the Sabi Sabi Resort. They were under attack by poachers who thought they found some gold, the Kruger Gold, if I'm not mistaken. They were being shot at before we got cut off. I've sent all the details to your secure account."

"Okay, what have you done?"

"I've had the locals notified, but it'll take time for them to reach the area. My concern is that they'll be taken hostage and moved somewhere off the grid. Can you use your resources to find them, perhaps track them, so we know where to look?"

"I'll see what I can do. I can't get there in time to do any good, and hostage rescue isn't my wheelhouse."

"How about our friends?"

Kane chuckled. "You're a mind reader, Hugh. I'll see what I can do and get back to you."

"I'm about to take off, so I probably won't be reachable until I land in Johannesburg."

"Understood. I'll make sure you have an update for when you arrive."

"Okay, thanks, Dylan."

"Good luck, Hugh. And when you find them, tell them to retire. They're not good for our health."

Reading laughed. "Something tells me they won't listen." He ended the call, turned off the phone to save the battery, then returned it to his pocket.

"Kruger Gold? If your friends have found that, they're going to be rich."

Reading didn't register for a moment that he was being spoken to, finally noticing the woman staring at him from the next seat, so far away due to the extra room he hadn't even realized she was there. "Excuse me?"

She smiled at him. "Sorry, I couldn't help but overhear. The Kruger Gold. Some say it could be worth over half a billion dollars today."

Reading's eyebrows popped. "Half a billion dollars? American dollars?"

She nodded.

"How do you know so much about it?" His eyes narrowed. "You're not an archaeologist, are you?"

She laughed, reaching over and placing a hand on his arm. "Oh, God no! I'm a model. But everyone in South Africa knows about Kruger's Gold."

Reading suddenly noticed the woman was striking. "Fashion model?"

She smiled.

Huh. Maybe first class isn't so bad after all.

He smiled, extending his hand. "Hugh Reading. And you are?"

Leroux & White Residence, Fairfax Towers

Falls Church, Virginia

"My God, that smells good! What are you making?"

Chris Leroux smiled at the sight of his girlfriend, Sherrie White, as she stood in the doorway of the kitchen wearing nothing but his t-shirt. "Damfino."

"Huh?"

"Damfino."

Her eyes narrowed. "Damned if I know?"

He grinned. "Exactly."

She shook her head, popping up onto the counter. "Okay, if *you* don't know, then I think we're in trouble."

Leroux lifted two hot dogs, split down the center, from the pan, placing them on the open half of a grilled cheese sandwich. "No, that's what they're called."

"Huh?"

"Damfino."

"They're called 'damned if I know'."

"Exactly."

Sherrie let out a frustrated burst of air. "Who's on first?"

"No idea, but if he wants a damfino, he better speak up." He placed another thick slice of old cheddar over the hotdog, then moved the second slice of buttered bread on top.

"I'm confused."

"Evidently." He decided he better save her, and spelled it out. "D-A-M-F-I-N-O."

Her eyes widened. "Damfino!"

"Exactly, as in 'damned if I know'. An old friend of the family showed me how to make them when he was visiting. Remember that friend of my dad's, Bob Crampton?"

"Oh, from San Diego?"

"Yeah, he and his folks had a Mel's Root Beer for a while. He invented the sandwich as a snack for himself, but when customers saw him eating it, they wanted it. Apparently, it was a hit."

Sherrie leaned over the glistening concoction still sizzling in the pan. "Looks terrible for you."

Leroux shrugged. "Anything that tastes good usually is."

Sherrie brightened. "Can I have one?"

Leroux nodded at a plate behind him. "Yours is already up."

She beheld the expertly plated sandwich, cheese oozing from the golden brown crusts, the curiously added hotdog demanding to be tasted. She took a bite and moaned. "Oh God, this is *so* good."

Leroux removed his own from the pan, sliding it onto the cutting board before slicing it at an angle. "I'll let Bob know you liked it."

Sherrie swallowed another bite as Leroux took his first. "Damfino. Where'd that come from?"

Leroux covered his mouth as he chewed. "The customers were asking what it was called, and he'd just say, damned if I know. It stuck."

"Hilarious!" She went to the fridge, pulling out a jug of milk. "So, what's on the agenda for today?"

Leroux gulped down his bite. "This is the first day off both of us have had together in a while, and we've already spent half of it sleeping in. I want to make the most of it." He took another bite, savoring the texture and flavors. "I was thinking non-stop sex."

Sherrie downed a long slug from her glass of milk before picking her sandwich up again. "I think you have to wait twelve hours after eating one of these."

Leroux quickly put down his plate. "Better to be safe."

Sherrie laughed, pointing at it. "Eat your damned sandwich, you'll get what's coming to you later. Today I want to go out and have some fun."

"Rollercoasters?"

She grinned. "That's an awesome idea! I haven't been on a rollercoaster in a dog's age."

Leroux reached for his plate. "So, umm, sex is off the table?"

Sherrie chewed another bite, covering her mouth. "Eat."

He shrugged. "Your loss." He took a bite, eyeing her the entire time. He loved her, and she loved him. There was no doubt about that. They had been together now for a couple of years, the reason for their initial union one they could never share with friends, she a CIA agent, he now an Analyst Supervisor. She had been assigned to tempt him—sexually—into spilling state secrets. He, the awkward shy geek, had somehow, miraculously, resisted her.

And ultimately charmed her.

It was his high school buddy, Dylan Kane, that had ultimately got them together despite his sense of betrayal when he had discovered the truth.

Something he could never thank his old friend enough for.

His phone vibrated on the counter. He glanced at the call display, the coded number raising his eyebrows.

Speaking of.

He swallowed, swiping a greasy thumb across the screen. "Hello?"

"Hey buddy, hope I'm interrupting some hanky panky."

"Apparently you have to wait twelve hours after eating a damfino."

"Oh, those things your dad's buddy used to make?"

"Yup."

Kane's voice became muffled, as if speaking to someone else. "Hey, babe? Do you know how to make a grilled cheese sandwich?"

"Not very popular in China."

"Okay, you're in for a treat. Do we have hotdogs?"

"What do you think?"

"Okay, get dressed. We're going shopping." There was a shuffling sound. "Okay, I'm back. The doc is in trouble again."

Leroux closed his eyes for a moment, shaking his head. "What now?"

"Apparently they're on safari in South Africa and ran into some trouble with poachers. I've sent you the details. See if you can get clearance to have a bird locate them. I'm guessing these guys will have them moved before the locals can respond, and if they're poachers, they're going to know all the good hiding spots."

Leroux headed for the bedroom to change. "Okay, I'll contact the director and get the okay."

"Good. And read the file. Apparently, the daughter of the Treasury Secretary is with them. That should grease some wheels."

"Okay, will do. I'll keep you posted."

"Do that. Now I have to go introduce Fang to one of the greatest culinary inventions of all time."

Greater Kruger National Park, South Africa

Acton sprinted as fast as he could for as long as he could, but it was no use. Despite the rough terrain, the poachers were soon out of sight. He slowed down, coming to a halt, hands on his knees as he gasped for breath.

"What are you waiting for?"

He turned his head to look up at Courtney, who appeared fresh.

Youth!

"Aren't you at least a little tired?"

She shrugged. "I run cross country at Harvard. The only difference here is it's in the dark, but once your eyes adjust, it's actually not that bad." She watched him, concerned. "Do you want me to run ahead?"

He shook his head, standing up straight and stretching his back. "No, we should stick together. There's a lot of things out here that would like to make a tasty snack out of you. They're less likely to attack if there're two of us."

This seemed to scare her and she stepped closer, warily scanning the grass that surrounded them, something he hadn't been doing enough of, his obsession with keeping as close as possible to Laura leaving him to neglect their own safety.

Courtney pointed to the horizon, a hill stretching toward the east. "That's pretty close, isn't it?"

Acton nodded. "Not too far. Why?"

"Well, we were up in that area yesterday, I think. There's no way a vehicle can go up that, it's too steep."

Acton eyed the silhouette of the hill. "So?"

"So, they would have to go around it."

Acton paused for a moment, truly listening to her for the first time. "What are you saying?"

"Well, if they went that way"—she pointed west of the hill—"then we'd still see their lights, right?"

Acton nodded, his mouth slowly opening as he realized what she was saying.

"So since we can't, they must have gone around it."

Acton smiled. "How high was it?"

She shrugged. "Not high. Maybe twenty or thirty feet, but steep enough that they'd have to go around it."

Acton's head bobbed. "But we can go over it."

"Exactly. It could save us a lot of time."

Acton handed her the backpack with their supplies. "Help out an old man, would you?"

Courtney gave a genuine smile, taking the backpack and slinging it over her shoulders. Acton adjusted the straps for her then gave the pack a yank.

"Okay, let's move!"

Operations Center 3, CIA Headquarters

Langley, Virginia

Chris Leroux held his palm to the scanner, a beam running down the display as every minute detail of his unique skin pattern was read by the computer then checked against the files of thousands of CIA employees. The security panel turned green with a beep, a click indicating the locks to the secure operations center assigned to his team had been unlocked. He stepped inside, his eyes quickly taking in the various pieces of intel displayed on the massive series of screens sweeping in an arc across the front of the room.

"What do we know?"

"Not much, sir," replied Sonya Tong, one of his top analysts. "State is definitely horny for intel, though. The director's already been in twice, and we just got authorization to retask a bird ten minutes ago."

"In position?"

"Thirty seconds," replied Randy Child, their newest and youngest member, a computer whiz kid with no filter between the brain and mouth.

"Has anything been confirmed by the locals?"

Tong shook her head. "Nothing yet. We don't even know if they've dispatched anyone."

Leroux spun toward her, his eyes narrowed. "What are the South Africans saying?"

"Nada. They're not answering."

"What?"

She shrugged. "The phone just goes to voicemail. This is all happening fast and it's the middle of the night there. Our liaison might be napping."

"Or taking a dump."

Leroux ignored Child's perfectly valid possibility. "So what have you done about it?"

Tong was prepared for the question, as he had expected her to be. "I've called the resort they were staying at and they've confirmed they're overdue. They're sending people out now to look for them."

"Did you warn them about the poachers?"

"Yes, but they seemed unconcerned."

"Brave or stupid," muttered Child.

Leroux agreed. "Yes, but either one gets boots on the ground."

"Bird's in position," announced Child.

"Okay, show me the resort." Child worked his terminal, a hazy green image appearing on the screen. "Okay, there's only one road into that place. Let's follow it, see what we see." The image scanned west, nothing but empty road and uninteresting landscape bordering it on either side.

And plenty of infrared signatures showing warm bodies, there so many it was likely all wildlife.

The door opened, Leroux's boss, National Clandestine Service Chief Leif Morrison, entered the room. Leroux kept his eyes on the display, not wanting to miss anything. "Sir, we're searching the road they were last reported on."

"Anything?"

"Not yet."

Something whipped past, Tong catching it first. "Stop!" She pointed at the screen, looking over at Child. "Back it up a bit, there was a vehicle off to the side."

Child rolled back the footage then zoomed in on what appeared to be some sort of off-road vehicle, lying on its side, a pulsating green emanating from the engine compartment indicating it had been recently running.

Leroux tensed slightly and he stepped closer, pointing to a patch of green at the bottom of the frame. "Reposition two meters south."

Child changed the angle, confirming Leroux's fears. What he had thought might be a pair of feet was confirmed, an entire body now visible, the heat signature rapidly fading as the cool night sapped the corpse's remaining body heat. "Looks like this is the place."

Tong pointed, her arm tracing the location of the body. "Could be the driver. Looks like he might have been pulled through the windshield."

Leroux nodded. "Could be."

Morrison stepped toward the screen. "Reposition to the rear of the vehicle."

Child tapped at his keyboard, a second image appearing beside the first, another body revealed. "Definitely the place."

Morrison turned to Leroux. "We need to identify them, now."

Leroux glanced at his boss. "Yes, sir, but there's no way we can do it from these images. Once the locals are on-scene, it should be quick."

"ETA?"

"No idea at this point. We're waiting to hear back from our liaison there."

"That's only two bodies. We know the Secretary's daughter was with three others, and the Actons were with another couple. Any sign of them? There should be at least eight plus their guide."

Leroux motioned to Child. "Zoom out from that area, look for any heat signatures."

Child complied, slowly expanding the view, the area alive with large animals, making it difficult to spot anything—this wasn't searching for a lone target in a barren desert.

Leroux shook his head, frustrated. "Sir, this is going to require boots on the ground."

Morrison nodded. "We've got a Delta unit over North Africa right now. They're being redeployed. Should be there by morning."

Leroux frowned. "That's a lot of time to hide them."

Morrison agreed. "Let's just hope this is a ransom situation and not a robbery."

"What do you mean?"

"If they think they're worth something alive, then they'll keep them that way. If they don't…"

Leroux stared at the two bodies on the screen. "They're dead."

"Exactly."

Somewhere over the Mediterranean Sea

"Zero-One, Control Actual. Come in, over."

Dawson jerked up in his seat as he activated his comm, surprised to hear from the Colonel. "Go ahead, Control."

"We're retasking your team. You're needed in South Africa."

"South Africa?"

His team fell silent.

"Yes, the Treasury Secretary's daughter is missing, presumed kidnapped by poachers."

Dawson pointed at Niner. "Have the pilot redirect to South Africa."

Niner nodded, heading for the cockpit. "Good thing we just refueled."

Dawson switched his comm back on. "What do we know?"

"All we know is that Professor Laura Palmer—"

Dawson's eyebrows shot up. "You're kidding me!"

"—nope, she and her husband are once again involved."

"Unbelievable."

"Some would say so, but they keep us entertained. Anyway, she called Interpol Agent Hugh Reading, who is the source of most of our intel at this time. Apparently, they were being pursued by poachers when they were cut off. Satellite imagery shows their vehicle overturned, with two bodies."

"Why were they with the Secretary's daughter?"

"Unknown. As far as we know they were *not* traveling together."

"When did this happen?"

"Less than an hour ago."

The plane banked sharply to starboard, Dawson reaching for a handhold as Niner returned, giving a thumbs up.

"Any contact with the hostiles?"

"Negative, no ransom demands yet, and we can't presume that's their motive. If they're poachers, this doesn't fit the profile."

"Why do we think they're poachers?"

"Apparently the professor used that term."

"It's rather specific."

"Agreed. Langley thinks someone in the vehicle may have known their attackers, perhaps the guide."

"Sounds like a good place to start the investigation. Have Langley find out if he had any family."

"Way ahead of you, Zero-One. Langley will be briefing you shortly."

"Copy that."

"Also, instructions have been sent to you through a secure message. We've got one pick up we need you to make on your way."

Dawson's eyes widened. "Sir?"

"Details are in the upload."

"Copy that."

"Oh, and BD?"

Dawson's eyes narrowed, the use of his moniker unusual over the comms.

And he knew what it was about.

"Did you find Maggie?"

Everyone stopped what they were doing, turning toward him.

"Yes."

The Colonel's voice was subdued, and Dawson already knew the answer to his next question. "Is she okay?"

"I'm sorry, BD, but the news isn't good."

Greater Kruger National Park, South Africa

Acton crept forward on his stomach, painfully aware of every scraping noise his body made against the hard rock beneath him. Courtney had been right, the hill steep and perhaps twenty-five feet high. And from the sounds he was hearing ahead, her guess that Tladi and his men had traveled around the hill, appeared accurate.

They had gotten lucky.

It had taken almost an hour for them to reach the hill at a jog, and he was exhausted, adrenaline the only thing keeping him from collapsing right now in a puddle of lactic acid and dehydrated tissues.

He inched forward some more.

And saw them.

Laura and the others appeared to be tied together to his right, about fifty feet away, the vehicles parked nearby, facing away from the rock face, as if in preparation for a hasty escape. Several tents were already set up along with a campfire, apparently no one concerned about the light.

And why should they be?

There was no one around for miles, and the only civilization was behind them, behind this large rock.

Come on Hugh, work your magic!

If he knew Reading, he would have immediately contacted his colleagues at Interpol to notify the South Africans, then he'd probably have his ass on a plane.

I hope he charged us for the flight.

Acton smiled.

And then he would have contacted Dylan.

Acton rolled onto his back, waving his arms back and forth at the sky, just in case there were any satellites or drones retasked due to his distinguished partner in this ordeal, the Treasury Secretary's daughter. He rolled back over, executing his birdcall once more, Laura flinching again.

I'm here, babe. Just stay alive.

Comforted in knowing she had received his message, he retreated the way he came, dropping to the ground, Courtney immediately at his side.

"Are they alive?"

"For now."

She hugged him, resting her head on his chest for a moment. "Oh, thank God." Then her shoulders slumped. "Why did they have to kill Dyson?"

Acton decided he better head off the tears and blame game about to happen. "They're murderers who don't value human life like we do. There's no one to blame except them."

"Yes there is," she mumbled. "He didn't want to come. He wanted to take some courses for extra credit. I forced him. I said if he didn't, we were over."

Acton grunted. "Young people—hell, old people—have been giving ultimatums to each other for time immemorial. You can't blame yourself. He died because of something *I* found, and somehow bad people found out."

She frowned. "If our car hadn't broken down, you wouldn't have had to pick us up, and he'd be alive."

Acton grinned. "There you go! Blame the Jag!" He took the backpack off her shoulder. "Let's get set up for the night." He pulled the tent out, choosing a spot near the side of the rock face, leaving one less direction anyone—or anything—might approach them from. Using the flashlight, he quickly read the instructions stitched onto the slipcase, then smiled. He removed the tent then tossed it a few feet away, it popping into shape, a shelter for two now at their service. He repositioned it, inserted the pegs, adjusted the guy lines, then stood up, satisfied. "We camp here for the night."

Courtney looked about. "Umm, aren't we a little close to them?"

Acton shook his head. "No, they've got no reason to look over here, and they'd have to climb that rock to do it. With the tent here, against the side, they don't really have the angle."

"But won't they see our fire?"

"We're not making one."

"But we'll freeze to death!"

"This is Africa, not Alaska. We'll be fine."

He unrolled two thin aluminized sleeping bags, handing them to her. "Here, zip these together so we can share body heat." Courtney took them and he turned his attention to transferring all their meager possessions inside the tent. Finished, he checked on her progress.

None.

He took over, quickly zipping the two bags together, then tossed them inside the tent. He held out his hand. "After you."

"Thanks." Courtney climbed inside and he followed, zipping the tent closed before inspecting it for any uninvited critters, finding none.

"Okay, we're good." He sat down on one side, cross-legged, pulling the backpack in front of him. He removed the emergency rations, cutting open the vacuum-sealed pack, pulling out what he assumed was jerky—whether it was beef was a question that would remain unanswered. He handed her some. "Eat."

She waved it off. "Not hungry."

He shoved his hand back toward her. "Eat. You'll need your strength."

She reluctantly took it, biting off a piece, her face scrunching up with disgust. "Eww, what is this?"

"Beef jerky. I think they call it biltong." Acton took a bite.

Not beef.

Courtney eyed it suspiciously. "Doesn't taste like it."

Acton lied. "It's just the seasoning. Eat it. It's protein and your body needs it." He poured out a cup of water from the canteen. "Don't waste a drop. We don't know when we'll be getting more."

Courtney grabbed it, downing most of it in one shot as she tried to rinse the taste of the jerky from memory. "That person your wife called. Will he help us?"

Acton swallowed, pushing past the taste. "Hugh won't rest until we're found." He took another bite then resealed the rest in the bag. Courtney handed the empty cup back and he refilled it, taking his own ration, savoring every sip like a fine wine before he screwed the cup to the top of the canteen. "Okay, let's get some sleep." He removed his hiking boots, placing them near the entrance, then climbed into the sleeping bag, turning his back to Courtney as she slid in beside him. "Good night."

"Good night."

He closed his eyes, images of Laura playing on the back of his eyelids as he said a silent prayer for the only woman he had ever truly loved. His eyes opened as he felt his companion cuddle up behind his back.

"Umm, is this okay?"

He grunted. "Sure, just don't get any ideas, I'm a married man."

"Eww! You're old enough to be my dad!"

"Ouch, that hurts."

He felt a hand rub his back gently. "Sorry, I was just joking."

He smiled slightly in the dark. "So was I. Now get some sleep. We need to be up before they are."

"Okay."

Road to Sabi Sabi Bush Lodge

Greater Kruger National Park, South Africa

Cashile frowned as he stared at the body of his friend, Sipho. They had known each other for years, Sipho the one who got him the job at the lodge, it the best job he had ever had.

He owed this man.

And now he would never pay him back.

"Where are the police?" he asked the others in frustration, but he already knew. They were at least an hour away, there an incident in town demanding the attention of the small force assigned to the area.

Missing tourists would have to wait.

Though now that they had confirmed deaths, including at least one murder, one would hope they might reprioritize.

He examined the ground with his flashlight, quickly spotting multiple tire tracks heading deeper into the park. "They went that way." He looked at the others. "We can't track them at night, we'll wait for dawn." He climbed into one of their vehicles. "Stay here until the police arrive. Make sure no one touches anything."

"Where are you going?"

"To tell his family. They'll want to know."

"Isn't his brother a bad one?"

Cashile nodded, Sipho on more than one occasion confiding in him about his great shame over how his brother had turned out. He considered it a personal failure, Sipho the eldest male of the family, responsible for the younger brother after their father had died. Yet despite his problems, he knew the man loved his brother, and would want him to know his fate. "Yes, but blood is blood. He'll want to know his brother is dead." He flinched, his satphone ringing in his pocket. He pulled it out and answered. "Hello?"

"Hi, my name's Chris. I was wondering if you could do me a favor."

Cashile's eyes narrowed, not sure who he was talking to. "What kind of favor?"

"I need you to take a picture of the two bodies and send them to me."

Operations Center 3, CIA Headquarters

Langley, Virginia

Leroux watched as the first face slowly appeared, the upload excruciating over the satphone of the lodge worker. Tong had called the resort, getting the number in the hopes they might get some intel now, rather than hours from now. It had been a brilliant idea, he expressing this, she blushing, her crush on him still in full bloom.

"We've got a forehead. Looks black."

Leroux muttered a curse under his breath at Child's observation. He had asked that the photo of the young man be sent first. They already knew who the other was, it confirmed by those on the ground. He turned to Child. "What do we know about this guy?"

"Nada beyond his name. He's got no record in our database, but I'm still trying to get access to the South African's."

"Still?"

"Yup. What can I say? No one's answering the phone."

Leroux dropped into his chair, growling in frustration. "This is ridiculous."

"You're telling me. Our interagency protocols say someone should be there, but for whatever reason, they don't seem to be tonight."

Leroux blasted a lungful of air through his nose. "Hack it."

Child gave a toothy smile. "I thought you'd never ask."

"Here comes the second photo," announced Tong, gesturing toward the screen. Leroux rose, there not enough detail yet for an identity, just a hairline visible. "Bring up the photos of her two male traveling companions." He already knew from the description the man on the other end had given, that the second body wasn't that of Professor Acton or his South African traveling companion, so they were operating under the assumption he was part of Courtney Tasker's traveling party.

Tong quickly had both images up, the newly arriving image in between, the forehead appearing.

"Do we have enough for facial recognition?"

Tong shook her head. "I need the eyes."

They appeared, closed and dead, Tong's fingers flying over the keyboard, a series of dots and lines appearing over the image as it continued to stream in. The superimposed data points flashed, along with those on the image to the left. She turned in her chair. "It's Dyson Bishop, sir."

Leroux sighed. "Okay, let the director know. Someone will want to notify the family."

Tong sent a message to Morrison's office as Leroux watched the rest of the image download.

Man, he was just a kid!

Another blast erupted from between his lips.

Please, God, let the others be okay.

Acton Camp

Greater Kruger National Park, South Africa

"Wake up!"

Acton grunted, Courtney shaking him by the shoulder. "What?" he groaned.

"Wake up!"

The growl on the other side of the impossibly thin tent had him bolt upright in an instant, a surge of adrenaline rushing through his veins as his body prepared for the crisis at hand, millions of years of evolution designed for this very moment.

He extricated himself from the sleeping bag, searching for the flashlight, finding it in Courtney's hands, it off, its purpose at the moment evidently that of a weapon. "Turn on the flashlight."

"Won't they see us?"

He raised his voice, hoping it might scare away what was probably a lioness or leopard—neither good prospects. "They're the least of our concerns right now." The light flicked on, it blinding, the sounds of their uninvited guest continuing unabated as it paced along the three exposed sides of the tent, its low growl signaling its intent—to nosh on a conveniently wrapped dinner.

He grabbed the gun, checking to make sure it was loaded, then handed her the knife. "If it comes through, I'll try to shoot it, but if I don't get it, use the knife to cut your way out of the tent and climb that rock. If it comes after you, go over the other side to their camp."

"Then I'll be their prisoner!"

"Yes, but you won't be eaten alive."

"But what about you?"

"I'll try to hold it off for as long as I can."

"But you'll die!"

"I'll be dead anyway if it gets in here. Better me than both of us."

Courtney's face twisted into one of emotional agony and she grabbed him around the neck, hugging him hard, this evidently her thing. "I'm so sorry I was ever mean to you."

He shrugged her off. "I need to be able to shoot. Now lie down flat against the back so you don't get in the way." He followed the sound of the great cat with the barrel of the gun, unable to see anything outside the tent, the decision to turn on the flashlight a mistake. "Turn that off," he said, nodding toward the light in her hand. She flicked it off and he rapidly blinked, trying to adjust, still relying on his ears as the predator paced outside their thin nylon shelter.

"Get out of here!" he yelled in the deepest, loudest voice he could manage, keeping as far back from the creature as he could, constantly shifting his position. Courtney scrambled to keep out of the way as he hoped the extra two or three feet might give him the split second he would need to take aim, rather than just fire. "Go on! Get out of here!"

Courtney was now yelling too, the fear in her quavering voice obvious as she shifted behind him, keeping her feet toward their hunter—and that's what it was, a hunter, there no doubt what they were in this equation—the prey.

And then there was silence.

"This is it!"

He took aim at where he thought it had stopped, saying a silent goodbye to Laura as a screeching growl erupted from the other side, four long slices of the night sky revealed as a claw tore open the tent.

He adjusted his aim as almost 300 pounds of nature's fury burst through the opening.

And fired.

Poacher's Camp

Greater Kruger National Park, South Africa

Laura bolted awake, the others, tied to her, waking as well. Her head spun toward where the man on watch had been stationed when she finally drifted off, finding him just waking up, judging from the amount of eye rubbing going on. The leader, the murderer, Tladi, climbed out of his tent.

"What was that?"

The watch shrugged. "Dunno. Gunshot?"

"From where?"

Another shrug. "Couldn't tell. It sounded close."

It had to be James. For some reason, he had needed to fire a gun, probably the rifle that had been in their vehicle, and she could think of only one reason—a lion or some other creature had attacked him.

It was a single shot, so it had either worked, and he was safe, or he hadn't been able to get off another shot, and he was being mauled to death at this very moment.

The thought nearly made her wretch.

She knew he was nearby. She had heard his birdcall, there no doubt in her mind it was him, he somehow having managed to follow them. It had sounded like it had come from above, atop the hill at their backs, he probably taking shelter on the other side, out of sight, but close.

If he were dying, these men could save him, though they might as easily kill him. Yet if he were as close as she thought he was, and being attacked by some animal, surely she would hear his cries.

And she heard nothing beyond what she had come to expect.

Tladi pointed at the top of the hill. "Go check it out."

The lookout hopped from his perch on the hood of one of the vehicles, Laura's heart hammering, debating what to do. If James were in trouble, they could help, but if he weren't, if he had survived the ordeal, then he was about to be discovered.

What do I do?

She made her decision, putting her faith in her husband, in his ability to survive. The single shot followed by silence had to mean he was alive and well.

Or already dead.

She cleared her throat. "It didn't come from there."

Tladi turned toward her. "What?"

She shoved her chin toward the open grassland in front of them. "It came from that direction."

Tladi's eyes narrowed. "How would you know?"

"I was awake, unlike your lookout."

The man glared at her then avoided eye contact with the boss.

"And why should I believe you?"

She shrugged. "You shouldn't, but I've got no reason to lie."

"Then why say anything?"

It was a question she hadn't anticipated, her heart skipping a beat as she thought of a reply. She nodded toward the lookout. "Because this idiot is supposed to be protecting *all* of us while we sleep, and he's not doing his job. Whoever fired that shot was probably protecting themselves from a lion or leopard. What if something had come along while he was sleeping? One of us could be dead right now. *You* could be dead right now."

Tladi stared at her for a moment then started screaming at the lookout in their native tongue, the man cringing with the onslaught.

Gorman leaned toward her. "He's saying that if he catches him asleep again, he'll feed him to the lions himself. You should be careful, he won't be too happy with you after this."

Laura kept an eye on the proceedings. "I don't care about that. We just need to survive a little longer."

"Why? Do you know something we don't know?"

She shook her head. "We just need to give Hugh time."

But it wasn't Reading that was going to save them, it was James, and she couldn't risk telling the others in case they slipped up and revealed the fact he was nearby.

She just prayed he was okay, and that the single shot she had heard was him coming out on top in the battle between man and nature.

Acton Camp

Greater Kruger National Park, South Africa

Acton lay gasping for breath, the massive creature's teeth inches from his throat, the stench of rotting meat overwhelming due to the animal's poor flossing regimen. Courtney lay draped over both of them, the knife buried to the hilt in its back, a lucky plunge piercing the chest cavity, between the ribcage.

They had survived.

And the warmth he felt around his waist was either him having pissed himself, or the rapidly flowing blood from the now dead creature thanks to a well-placed shot to the upper-chest.

"Get off me," he grunted, Courtney scrambling toward the back of the tent as if she had just realized what she was lying on. He strained against the weight, trying to roll the massive beast off him with no luck. He stared at Courtney, hugging her knees behind him. "A little help?"

She darted forward, her adrenal glands evidently pegged, and put both hands on the torso, pushing hard. Together they rolled the creature off, Acton finally pulling free. Grabbing the flashlight, he flicked it on, quickly confirming it was absolutely dead and not just in shock, then flicked it off.

"No! Leave it on!"

He held a bloody finger up to her lips. "Shhh. There's no way they didn't hear that shot. Stay completely quiet and listen." He strained through the pounding in his ears to hear anything outside that might suggest they were about to be discovered, but heard nothing. "Okay, we need to move, and move quickly."

"Why?"

"Because we've got a three hundred pound meal sitting here that every carnivore for miles is going to be smelling."

"What do we do?"

He unzipped the tent, looking about in case the lioness had brought friends, then spotting nothing, grabbed the hind legs and pulled, Courtney soon helping. Clear of the tent, Acton scrambled back inside, reloaded the gun, then checked his boots for uninvited guests before putting them back on, doing the same for Courtney's before handing them to her. "Always check."

She nodded, checking again before jamming her feet into her sneakers. Acton grabbed their gear, stuffing it into the backpack, then packed up the tent, the entire endeavor taking less than five minutes.

"Where do we go?"

Acton had already been thinking about that very question, coming to a decision moments before. He pointed farther along the hill. "That way. If they're going to investigate, they'll come either over or around. This way will give us some warning."

Courtney slung the backpack over her shoulders, Acton taking the lead with the rifle at the ready as they broke out into a jog, the night sky lighting their way, Acton's biggest concern still not the poachers on the other side of the hill, but the fact they were both covered in blood, the scent of which was rapidly spreading.

This day just keeps getting better and better.

University College London Dig Site
Lower Nubia, Egypt

Leather checked his watch. Their chopper was another hour out. It would take them to Aswan where a private jet would be waiting, Laura Palmer part of a fractional private jet network, there a member aircraft in Cairo. He had just finished briefing Mitchell and his wife on what was going on when his satphone vibrated. He pulled it off his hip as Warren Reese, one of his trusted men, walked up to him.

"I've packed everything we should need. Are you sure the two of us is enough?"

Leather checked the call display. "Palmer would never agree to leave the students with any less protection. You and I can coordinate with the locals." He took the call. "Leather."

"Hey, Colonel, need a lift?"

His eyes narrowed, trying to place the voice that definitely sounded familiar. "Excuse me?"

"Look up."

He tilted his head back and spotted a flashing beacon overhead, the rectangle of an open chute visible, and above that, the red and green running lights of an airplane. "Who is this?"

"A friend from the jungles of Brazil and the volcanoes of Iceland."

Leather smiled, finally recognizing the voice of Burt Dawson, leader of the Delta team he had the pleasure of working with on several occasions. "Just how the hell are you planning on landing that thing here?"

There was a laugh that made him nervous. "We're not landing. See the chute?"

"Yes."

"Retrieve the supplies and set yourself up for pickup. How many can you add to our merry band?"

"Two."

"Sounds good. We'll see you soon."

The call ended as two of Leather's men peeled away in one of the camp's vehicles, rushing toward where the supply drop was touching down.

"What do you think it is?" asked Reese, a smile spreading across Leather's face as he realized what was going on.

"Oh, I know what it is."

Reese finally figured it out and groaned. "Bloody hell, you're not telling me—"

"Yup, Skyhook."

Reese's groan grew louder. "Ugh, I've managed to avoid that my entire career."

Leather slapped him on the back, deciding to have some fun with him. "Just remember to squeeze your cheeks. You don't want to shite your pants."

The jeep returned and the equipment was unloaded, lights in the camp flooding the area, every student now out of bed, few able to sleep after hearing their professor was in trouble, none with all the commotion. His men set up the system, the balloon quickly inflating then floating into the air as Leather and Reese climbed into their harnesses, snapping onto the lift line.

Leather looked at Reese. "Ready?"

"Cheeks squeezed."

Leather laughed. "Good." He nodded at his men holding the balloon in place. "Let it go." The balloon soared into the air, beacons flashing, the sound of the transport aircraft overhead changing as it banked, the pilot having spotted the lights.

"Good luck," said Mitchell. "Bring her back safe."

Leather nodded, doing one last check as the plane roared overhead, his equipment bag lying at his feet, latched to his harness. He heard the yoke on the front of the plane catch the cable stretched between the balloon and themselves, and braced.

"Squeeze!"

He was ripped from the desert floor and yanked into the air, the force tremendous, enough to leave him gasping from the shock. He peered down and saw Reese below him, the plane gaining altitude, already redirecting toward their destination as the crew inside reeled them in.

I love this job!

Operations Center 3, CIA Headquarters

Langley, Virginia

"Sir, the drone is coming online now."

Leroux rose from his chair, stepping toward the screen, most of it displaying the footage from the drone that had just arrived from a covert CIA installation in Burundi. "Anyone see anything?"

"There's too much wildlife," complained Tong, and she was right. The brief imagery they had received from the satellite was still being analyzed by his team, so far they finding nothing, the area simply too vast with thousands of creatures similar in size to humans.

And it appeared the drone footage was going to be the same.

"Okay, start a standard search pattern from their last known location. We'll find them."

Child let out a burst of joy. "I'm in!"

Leroux smiled, stepping over to Child's workstation. "What have you got?"

Child's fingers attacked the keyboard. "The guide has a record from years ago, apartheid era—"

"Everybody has a record from back then."

"Exactly. He's been clean for over twenty years."

Leroux nodded, exactly as he had expected. A resort of the quality the Actons and Courtney Tasker would stay at would have thoroughly vetted their staff. "Family?"

"At least three brothers with records, but get this"—he gestured at the display, an image appearing of a disagreeable-looking man in his thirties. "This is his brother, Tladi. He's got several recent charges against him, and according to the file, is suspected of poaching, though they haven't been able to nail him for it yet."

Leroux grunted. "Well, that's quite the coincidence."

Child glanced up at him. "And we don't believe in coincidences?"

Leroux smiled. "No, *we* don't." He jabbed a finger at the screen. "Get that info to Agent Reading. He can check it out with the locals when he arrives."

"You don't want Delta on it?"

Leroux shook his head. "Sometimes the scalpel is better than the hammer. Besides, if it *is* him, then he's somewhere out there"—he motioned at the drone footage—"not sitting at home."

Greater Kruger National Park, South Africa

Acton held up a fist, coming to a stop.

"What?"

"Shhh." He strained to pick up what he thought he had heard, and as his heart steadied, it came into focus.

Running water.

He pointed ahead. "I'm hearing water." He glanced back, there no sign of pursuit, human or otherwise, and they were now at least a good mile from the campsite. They should be safe, though not here.

Water meant animals, animals meant prey, prey meant more of what they had just gone through.

But water also meant they could wash the blood off themselves, perhaps reducing the chances of another encounter. He continued cautiously forward, stopping at the edge of a stream, small enough there wouldn't be anything lurking in the waters, waiting for them, yet big enough to work with.

"Okay, you first. Strip everything off that has blood on it, then wash it as best you can."

"You're not going to look, are you?"

Acton rolled his eyes. "You've got nothing I haven't seen before, but don't worry, I'll be busy watching your back."

"Huh?"

He jabbed a finger at the darkness. "Your back, figuratively, not literally."

"Oh." She quickly peeled off her top, her pants apparently fine, then dropped to her knees, shoving the shirt in the water as Acton watched the surrounding area for hostiles, saying nothing. She began to hum a tune, a few murmured words escaping.

"What's that?"

"A little Kanye."

Acton groaned.

"Not a fan?"

"That's putting it mildly."

"Well, you're old, so you're not supposed to like him."

Acton tilted his head to the side for a second, nodding, the girl right.

"Did you know he might run for president?"

Acton almost looked at her in shock. "God help us."

She giggled. "I know, right? Like, I like his music, but wow, he'd be like a disaster, right?"

Acton paused, squinting at something in the distance.

Bush.

"The scary thing is he could win."

Acton's eyebrows popped at that statement, looking down at the girl.

She caught him. "Hey, you said you wouldn't look."

His head spun away. "Sorry, you just shocked me with that. How the hell could he win?"

"Well, he's got like twenty-five million Twitter followers, and with his wife and her family, they've got like almost every young person in America following them. If they decide to vote, he wins."

"Perish the thought."

"I know, right?" She tossed her shirt on the ground beside her, bending over and rinsing her face and arms.

Acton shook his head. "That's the problem today. Western culture loves its celebrities so much, they actually believe they're smarter than them because they have a platform. I forget who said it, but youth and beauty aren't accomplishments, but today's youth thinks it is. They think if someone is a star then they must be smart, so should be listened to."

Courtney put her shirt back on, turning toward him. "Wasn't Ronald Reagan an actor?"

Acton gave her a look. "Please tell me you're not comparing Ronnie to Kanye."

"No, just sayin', an actor became president, so why not a rapper?"

Acton pointed at their surroundings. "Watch for any movement. Keep scanning the entire area. You see something, you let me know."

She gestured toward the gun. "You giving me that?"

He paused.

"Come on! I'm an excellent shot."

He sighed, handing it over. She had done well in the tent, attacking the lioness with her knife rather than running off and leaving him there. After the way she had acted before, he had expected her to simply sit there screaming while he tried not to become dinner.

She turned her back as he stripped to his underwear, everything on him covered in blood.

"Would you vote for him?"

She glanced at him, her eyes locking on his body. He looked up at her as he plunged his pants into the stream. "Hey, I thought we agreed to no looking."

She turned away. "Umm, sorry, I uh, didn't realize you were, you know?"

"What? So old?"

"No!" she gushed, turning back toward him. "Buff!" She tore her eyes away. "Your wife's a lucky woman."

Acton smiled, shaking his head as he worked on his clothes. "I like to think so. And you didn't answer the question. Would you vote for him?"

She shook her head. "My daddy has too many guns in the house for me to risk it."

Acton chuckled. "I guess that explains why you're handy with a weapon. What about your friends?"

She shrugged as Acton moved on to his shirt. "Oh God, enough of them are stupid enough to do it just because they'd think it was funny."

Acton washed the blood off his face and arms. "Sometimes I think there should be a test before you're allowed to vote."

Courtney laughed. "Yeah, but I'd probably fail. So would most of my friends. The news just isn't interesting, and there's too much going on now. From the moment I wake up to the moment I go to sleep, my phone is going off constantly with text messages, Snapchat, Facebook, Twitter, Instagram, whatever. I barely have a moment to myself anymore."

Acton stood, shoving his feet into his pant legs. "I wouldn't want to be a kid today."

Courtney glanced at him, her eyes lingering again. He jabbed a finger at the darkness. She quickly complied. "No, it sucks. Sometimes I'd like to just smash my phone so I could get a little peace, but then I'd be piled on by all my so-called friends for being antisocial." She sighed. "You just can't win."

Acton put his boots on. "Perhaps you should start pruning your friends list."

She spun, gaping at him. "Are you kidding? The number of followers you have is like a status symbol. If I got rid of the people I didn't really know, I'd have like, I don't know, maybe twenty friends?"

"How many do you have?"

She shrugged, handing him the gun. "I don't know, a few thousand on Facebook, tens of thousands on Twitter and the others."

Acton shook his head. He didn't have a Twitter account, didn't know what Instagram and Snapchat were—and more importantly didn't care—and had six friends on Facebook, everything set to private so he wasn't discoverable. He had too much going on in his life where he dealt with people face-to-face, like it was meant to be. He wasn't about to waste any of it in the virtual world.

He pointed to the backpack. "Let's try to wash the tent out, then we'll get moving." Something growled in the distance. "And let's be quick about it."

Poacher's Camp

Greater Kruger National Park, South Africa

Tladi leaned back in his seat, waiting for dawn, dreaming of what a mountain of gold could do for his station in life. But fantasy was one thing, too much of his life spent daydreaming of what could be, rather than what was. It was why he stole, it was why he poached. Working hard in Belfast meant little pay, a sore back, and a hard life.

None of that interested him.

Until yesterday, the only fast-track to bettering his position was through crime, poaching the only way he could see his way to the big time.

But lost gold?

He had heard of the Kruger Gold. Everyone had. Though it was just a legend. Or so he had thought. Yet now these rich people said it was real, and Florence's father even had one of the coins. If one coin existed, then others must.

But he had been disappointed before.

He needed more information.

He grunted at one of his men. "Bring her to me."

His man nodded, jogging over to the prisoners and cutting her loose. He led her by the arm, roughly, something Tladi had no problem with.

She glared at him, appearing tired and thirsty, yet still feisty.

I like that.

He might just have to have a little fun with her before killing her.

Because she *was* going to die.

They all were.

Though not until he had his gold.

He stared at her chest for a moment, then at her face. "You said it was in a mine."

She nodded.

"And you don't know where."

"No."

"But my brother did."

"Yes."

"Why do you think it's in a mine?"

"We found several coins with a piece of coal wrapped inside a jar." She pulled something from her pocket, carefully unwrapping it. He leaned forward in anticipation. "We think it was left as a clue to where the gold was hidden."

Tladi's eyes narrowed with disappointment, roughly grabbing the piece of rock. He held it up. "Are you kidding me? You think you've found a treasure missing for over one hundred years because you found a piece of rock wrapped up in a jar?"

The woman shrugged. "That's how archaeology works. You process a site, make a hypothesis, then try and prove it. Quite often you can't because of the amount of time that has passed. We've made a hypothesis, and now we need to try and prove it."

He had no clue what this hypothesis word meant, though it sounded an awful lot like a guess. He held up the stone. "My brother died for this." He threw it away, the woman yelping and rushing over to grab it. Jacob beat her to it as he walked over to join them.

"Looks like coal." He tossed the rock to the woman, who caught it, carefully rewrapping it before returning it to her pocket. "What's so important about that?"

"She thinks it's a clue to where the gold could be."

Jacob's head bobbed. "Could be."

Tladi's eyes narrowed. "What do *you* know about it?"

"I worked in the mines when I was younger."

Tladi felt hope returning, however faint. "Where can it be found?"

"Lots of places, I guess. There're mines all over the place."

Tladi frowned. "Then what good is that?" He leaped to his feet, startling the woman. He pointed at her pocket with the rock. "My brother died for a piece of rock that can be found anywhere. How the hell are we supposed to find some treasure based on that?" He shook his head, rage building from within at the thought of his brother, dead because of these rich, privileged people. "I say we kill them and cut our losses."

"But why?" cried the woman. "We've done nothing wrong. We don't know who you are! Just let us go!"

Tladi wagged a finger at her. "We've been over this already. You know Sipho was my brother."

"We won't say anything, I swear."

Tladi smiled, pulling his gun. "Of course you won't. You'll be dead."

Second Acton Camp

Greater Kruger National Park, South Africa

Acton positioned the torn portion of the tent against the rock face, a concave in the stone fitting it almost perfectly. He followed Courtney inside, zipping the entrance shut behind them, once again using the flashlight to search for uninvited guests, guests they wouldn't be able to keep out thanks to the now disturbingly obvious claw marks.

"Make sure you check your shoes in the morning."

"Okay." Her eyes widened. "What if I have to pee? You made me drink an awful lot of water."

Acton climbed into the sleeping bag, Courtney following. "I wanted us super-hydrated. We don't know when we'll get access to more water, and it'll also act as an alarm clock."

"Huh?"

"Ancient Native American trick. We'll sleep for a few hours then we'll wake up because we need to pee. That will give us a jump-start on the others."

She snuggled up behind him once again. "Do you really think you can save them?"

Acton closed his eyes. "Not at all. But I have friends who can, and they'll need to know where they are."

"But how will they find *us*?"

Acton smiled, pointing toward the sky. "I have friends in high places."

Operations Center 3, CIA Headquarters
Langley, Virginia

"We might have found them."

Director Morrison stared at the display as he entered the Operations Center, joining Leroux in the middle of the room as footage from a UAV showed a large group of almost twenty people. "What makes your famous gut think it's them?"

Leroux flushed slightly. "Because of this." He motioned and Child brought a second image up showing two heat signatures in what appeared to be a tent.

"Where's this?"

"On the other side of this hill."

"So? Could just be a couple of campers."

"Not allowed. Besides, they've got no fire set or any other heat source. I'm thinking they're following the other group and are using the hill as a blind."

Morrison nodded slowly. "Thin."

"Yup, but we've got some evidence."

"I hope so."

Leroux glanced at Child. "Zoom in on the large group." The image filled the screen, Leroux stepping closer, pointing at five people lined up against the hillside. "These look like our hostages."

Morrison joined him. "There's only five. I thought our intel said there's at least seven—three surviving members of Ms. Tasker's group, the Actons, and their two companions." His jaw slowly dropped. "Ahh, so you think these other two off on their own are the missing hostages."

"Exactly." He gestured to Child. "Then there's this."

Satellite footage from earlier appeared. Morrison stepped closer, his eyes narrowing. "What the hell am I looking at?"

Leroux chuckled as a man lay on his back, waving his arms at the sky. "Once we knew where to look, we went back and reviewed the satellite footage. We found this."

Morrison shook his head, turning to Leroux. "Who do you think it is?"

"It has to be Professor Acton. From the size, it's clearly male, and he's the only male in the group that might actually think he'd be under surveillance of some type."

Morrison chuckled. "I hope he doesn't think we have a satellite on him at all times."

"Perhaps we should," muttered Child. "He's like a walking magnet for trouble."

Morrison grunted. "Not in the budget, but not a bad idea." He motioned to the image showing the two targets in a tent. "So, it's probably safe to assume they're not locals or law enforcement, and no tourist would think to wave hello at us, so let's assume it's Acton and someone else. Who's the second target?"

"We're thinking Laura Palmer."

"That would make sense. But if it is, what are they doing? If they've escaped, why not seek help?"

Leroux glanced at his boss. "You know them. They chronically do the right thing."

Morrison sighed. "Some people shouldn't be allowed out of the country." He waved his hand at the screen. "Okay, so the professors are following the others, and Acton is assuming he's being watched by us, so he followed them so that we'd know where to look. Ballsy, but his job is done. Any way to let him know?"

Leroux shook his head. "We have no way to communicate with them beyond visual, and that could be seen by the hostiles. They might kill the hostages and flee the area."

Morrison cursed. "Then what can we do?"

"Keep them under surveillance so Delta knows exactly where to go when they arrive.

Morrison frowned. "And pray whatever information that's keeping them alive is still worth it by then."

Child cleared his throat. "Sir, something's happening." He pointed at the footage showing the group as the drone came back into position. One of the hostages was no longer with the others, and it appeared that a gun was being held to their head.

Morrison frowned. "I hate it when I'm right."

Poacher's Camp

Greater Kruger National Park, South Africa

Laura closed her eyes, drawing in a slow, deep breath as Tladi raised his pistol, aiming it directly at her forehead. A million things went through her mind, and she felt herself begin to shut down, her brain mentally preparing for the inevitable. She thought of her parents, of her late brother, of her students, but mostly of James, and how devastated he'd be.

Goodbye, my love!

Yet she refused to make things easy, instead opening her eyes and staring at her killer. This bastard would live with the image of what he had done, her glare boring into him, the memory of the woman who refused to give into fear, something he would live with forever.

You'll remember my face until the day you die.

She only hoped it would be soon, and knowing James, it would be. He wouldn't rest until she was found, until the others were saved, then he'd make sure justice was delivered, if not by his hand, then by those they knew.

Dylan will probably be the one.

"I wonder if he meant the old Rhodes Mine."

Tladi's wrist flicked to the side, the gun pointed away from her as he stared at the former miner. "What?"

"You know, the Rhodes Mine. It's about five kilometers from here. It's been abandoned for as long as I can remember. Before the wars, I think."

Tladi stared at Jacob. "Why that and not another one?"

Jacob shrugged. "Well, most of the mines in the area were still being worked until after the park was founded. If the gold had been hidden there, surely it would have been found. You can't keep a secret that big. And besides, didn't she say Sipho said it was close? It's the closest I know of, and the only one I know of that mined coal around here."

Tladi's head bobbed and Laura's chest relaxed slightly, the man possibly onto something. Then tightened again with the realization that if he were right, the need for her and the others was about to disappear.

Tladi lowered his weapon. "Do you know how to get there?"

Jacob shrugged. "Sure, at least I think so. My dad pointed it out to me when I was a boy. Said I should be grateful I didn't work there. Apparently, it was quite the hellhole."

Tladi quickly raised the weapon again, pointing it at her forehead. "I guess I don't need you, then."

Laura met his stare and shrugged. "Assuming it isn't well hidden, then no, you don't."

His eyes narrowed, the gun listing to the right once again. "What do you mean?"

"I mean, I'm an archaeologist. This is my area of expertise. Do *you* know how to properly explore an abandoned mine? How to prevent a cave-in? How to spot changes in the soil or the walls that would suggest something hidden behind it?" Tladi remained silent, though the gun continued to drift away, albeit slowly. "In the off chance you don't, it'll be a lot quicker and a lot safer with me leading the way."

Tladi nodded slowly. "You're right. That means I need *you*, not the others." He spun on his heel, walking toward the hostages huddled against the hillside. She rushed after him, avoiding the outstretched arm of the miner, and put herself between the others and Tladi. "Touch a hair on their heads, and I'll make sure the entire cave collapses on your murdering ass."

Tladi smiled at her. "I like you. When this is done, you're not going to like the party I throw with you as the feature attraction." His chin jutted toward the young girl. "And you're invited too."

Laura quavered inside as the young woman buried her head in her boyfriend's shoulder, but wouldn't give the bastard the satisfaction of knowing the prospect terrified her.

Though she did take some comfort knowing help was on the way, and the longer she could keep everyone alive, the more likely they were to be saved.

Before this day is over, you'll be dead, and we'll be downing beers in celebration.

Approaching South African Airspace

"What's her status?"

Dawson stood near the cockpit where his pacing had taken him while waiting for an update about Maggie. It had been hours, the pickup of Leather and his man long completed, and his entire team was on edge, everyone concerned for her wellbeing, and for their friend's.

"It looks like she had a stroke of some type, the doctor's aren't sure yet," replied Red.

Dawson's eyes closed and his shoulders sank as he dropped into the first seat he could find. He let out a slow breath, his chest hurting. "Is it related to what happened in Paris?"

"They don't know yet, but it could be."

"What about that drug? Isn't there something that they inject or something?"

"They gave it to her, but it has to be administered within four hours. They don't know when she suffered the stroke. She was missing for over half a day."

Dawson punched the armrest with his free hand as he processed this new reality. He had thought she was dead in Paris, and it had sent him into a rage, killing every Muslim attacker in sight before his team had hauled him onto the plane. The discovery she was alive had made him realize how much he truly loved this woman, a woman who had forced herself into his life at the urging of the other Unit wives. Her recovery had been slow but complete—or so he had thought.

Had she not been telling him something?

Had she been given bad news by the doctors at her recent appointment?

He knew there was something she wasn't telling him, and he had assumed it was so that he wouldn't worry, though something like this, something as important as this, he couldn't imagine her not sharing with him. After all, they were to be husband and wife, and husbands and wives didn't keep secrets that big from each other.

He sighed, leaning his head back in the chair, his eyes closed. "So what you're saying is it might not work."

"I'm sorry, BD. I wish it were better news."

Dawson gripped the armrest, his knuckles turning white. "There has to be something they can do!"

The others, who had been giving him some privacy, looked at him for a moment before returning to what they were doing.

"She's in good hands, and she's not alone. Shirley and the others are all here, and so are Spock and Sweets. She won't be alone, I promise you. And the moment I hear something, I'll let you know."

Dawson's head dropped forward, his heart pounding as he struggled to maintain control, the realization he may not know for hours what was happening to the most important person in his life, setting in. "We're about to land. You'll have to route any updates through Control for operational integrity." He leaned forward. "Do whatever it takes, Red. I can't lose her. If there's a doctor that can help her, you get him. I don't care where he is or what it costs. Do whatever it takes."

"You can count on it, BD."

Dawson ripped the headset from his ear and rose, marching silently past the others toward the bathroom on the comfort pallet, snapping the door shut behind him, the lights flickering on automatically. His clenched fists shoved against the wall on either side of the mirror as he stared at himself, his face beet red, his eyes burning with tears that threatened to escape their confines, the veins in his neck throbbing as the pressure built.

A roar escaped from within, the balls of his fists slamming against the wall several times, the entire interior rattling from the force before he finally dropped his throbbing hands to the counter surrounding the tiny sink, sucking in deep, rapid breaths as he struggled to regain control.

He stared at himself again.

She's in good hands and you've got a mission. There's nothing you can do to help her except clean up this mess and get back home.

There was a knock at the door.

"Hey, BD, you okay?"

It was Atlas. Dawson turned the tap on, splashing water on his face and rubbing the back of his neck. "Yeah, give me a minute."

"Okay, buddy, I'll be right here if you need me."

"Copy that." Dawson splashed more of the cool water on his face, beginning the slow, rhythmic breathing he had been taught, bringing his heart rate under control, calming himself. He grabbed some paper towels from the dispenser and dried off, then pulled open the door, nodding at a concerned Atlas.

But this was no time for concern.

They had a mission, and his personal problems were not the nation's.

Lives were depending on him keeping it under control, and that's what he would do.

Maggie would have to wait.

No matter how much the thought tortured his soul.

Second Acton Camp

Greater Kruger National Park, South Africa

Acton woke, his bladder demanding attention.

Gotta love those Natives.

He looked about, it still dark outside, though it was evident the sun was about to crack the horizon. Courtney lay beside him, gently snoring, clearly as exhausted as he was, despite her youth. The pampered lifestyle she probably lead compared little to the rough one he was used to, two decades of crawling in, around and under every manner of dig and discovery, kept you in shape—no matter what the age.

He checked then donned his boots before unzipping the tent and stepping outside, surveying the surroundings, the rifle gripped in his hand. Nothing seemed to be in the immediate vicinity, at least nothing with an obvious appetite. He walked about a hundred feet from their tent and relieved himself, the Native alarm clock having worked as planned.

He stuck his head in the tent. "Rise and shine!"

Courtney groaned in protest. "Just a few more minutes!"

He slapped her feet poking up at the end of the sleeping bag. "No time to waste. Get up, check your shoes, then do whatever you need to do to your bladder and bowels. We're out of here in five."

"Ugh, you're disgusting."

"Hey, just because you're rich doesn't mean you don't shit like the rest of us, unless of course you're Kim Jong-un."

Courtney stopped in mid-effort of extricating herself from the sleeping bag. "Huh?"

Acton spun his hand, urging her on. "The party line is that he works so hard, he burns everything he puts into his body, so there's no waste to get rid of."

"You're kidding me! I thought that was just in the movie The Interview."

Acton chuckled. "Where do you think they got the idea from?" He looked at her. "I'm surprised you saw that."

She reached for her shoes, finally out of the sleeping bag. "My daddy said it was my patriotic duty to see the movie because the North Koreans said we shouldn't and a bunch of pussy—his word, not mine—liberal Hollywood types were too scared to exercise their First Amendment right to free speech."

Acton smiled. "Sounds like your dad and I might get along."

She shook her head. "Nah, he thinks if you're a teacher then you've just failed at what you studied to do in real life."

Acton chuckled. "Sounds like quite the guy." His hand darted forward, batting the shoe out of her hand as she was about to shove her foot inside.

"Hey!"

He pointed at the shoe now on the other side of the tent. "Did you check that?"

She glared at him then grabbed the shoe, tipping it over and making a show of tapping the toe to shake anything loose.

A massive huntsman spider dropped out and she screamed, diving past Acton and outside the tent. Acton laughed, picking the innocent creature up and carrying it outside. He placed it on the ground near the hillside about twenty feet away, though not before ordering a still panicking girl to be quiet.

A hand slapped over her mouth, muffled shouts still audible for a few moments more.

Acton pointed to the tent. "Finish getting ready."

She nodded, entering the tent tentatively, and he smiled as he saw her warily checking both shoes, twice, before slipping them on. She emerged a few moments later. He pointed to an outcropping about fifty feet away. "You can do your business there. I can't see you, but I can see anything approaching. Just call if you need help."

"O-okay." She rushed away from their camp, her scare apparently upping the urgency of her need.

Poacher's Camp

Greater Kruger National Park, South Africa

Tladi smiled slightly as he relaxed in the back seat of his prized Nissan, though as his eyes took in what hours ago had been a testament to his growing success, he pictured even greater decadence.

A Range Rover!

He shook his head, easing back on the threadbare cloth, his eyes closing.

Might as well be a Jag. Can't trust it.

A smile spread across his face.

A Jeep Wrangler Rubicon!

His head bobbed slowly as he pictured riding through the streets of Belfast, music blaring, his posse with him as they ruled the town he had grown up impoverished in, all thanks to his father abandoning them.

He frowned as he thought of his brother.

A brother who was wrong.

He wasn't too young to remember. He had been there when his father had died, and he remembered the night as if seared to the back of his eyelids.

But it was easier to blame the choices he had made on a man that couldn't defend himself, than to accept responsibility.

And it was even easier to blame a man you pretended had abandoned you, rather than died fighting for his last breath, not wanting to leave his family on their own in a world that could be cruel to a fatherless household.

I'll take care of them, father.

And he would. He wasn't heartless. If they indeed found the gold, it would change everything. He would make sure his entire family never went hungry again, nor those of his friends. It would change things for all of them.

And he'd have respect, respect for the first time in his life.

And maybe even some self-respect.

He sighed. It would solve all their problems, this gold.

And not only would he be rich, he'd be the most powerful man in town.

He smiled.

I'll buy the town!

He would build the biggest house, have a fleet of cars, the finest clothes and jewelry, and fill his days with booze and women—and kick his wife out the door if she had a problem with it.

It would be legendary, the ultimate fantasy come true, and it was so close he could taste it.

An elephant trumpeted in the distance.

And I'll get better guns.

He loved poaching, loved the thrill of the hunt, and loved the payday in the end. It was hard work, dangerous work, which was why he had been reluctant to get into it at first, though once he had seen the potential for himself, the dangers had been forgotten, the thrill of the chase, of the risk of being caught, simply too impossible to resist.

He'd keep poaching, no matter the result at the end of today's journey.

It would simply be different.

Better guns, better vehicles, better equipment, more ammo, and no need to take what was so valuable on the black market.

He'd simply enjoy the hunt, then move on.

And if he were caught, he'd have more than enough money to bribe his way out of the situation.

He sighed, his smile spreading as he opened his eyes, the sun cracking the horizon, it soon time to go. He sat upright, stretching, once again running on adrenaline now that he knew there might be a possibility of finding the famous lost gold.

And when he did, when that first piece was in his hands, he would avenge his brother's death, and kill every last one of these privileged white people and their lackeys trying to pose as equals.

Approaching South African Airspace

"Zero-One, Control."

Dawson drew a deep breath, getting back into game mode. The guys had pretty much left him alone for the past hour, their attempt to give him space unfortunately allowing him to dwell on his thoughts, the imagination a horrible thing when it had few facts to go on.

But that had to end.

Maggie had to be secondary—he had a job to do, and lives depended on it.

"Go ahead, Control."

"Bad news, Zero-One"—his heart nearly stopped, his eyes closing as he prepared for the news of Maggie's death—"the South African government has given you permission to land and search for our people, but unarmed only."

A sigh of relief escaped, this very moment proving why people in his business didn't go on ops when there was a personal crisis underway at home. Yet there was no choice, his team the only one in the region that could be retasked. He could step aside, let Atlas lead the team, but that would leave them a man down, and if something happened to them because of it, he'd never be able to live with himself.

Get it together. Shut this shit down!

"Repeat that, Control."

"No weapons, Zero-One."

He shook his head. "Control, you expect us to go up against a dozen armed poachers with what, white flags?"

"Don't shoot the messenger, Zero-One. This is from State."

Dawson frowned. "Can we do what we usually do? Gear up at the embassy?"

"Negative, Zero-One. The South Africans are wise to that one. You're to find our people then report their location to the South Africans so they can deal with it."

"Is that State's line?"

"Zero-One, Control Actual." Dawson sat straighter as the Colonel joined the conversation. "Negative, that's State's line to the locals. You do what you need to do to bring our people home, but you'll have to walk off that plane unarmed, and any US issue weapons or gear are forbidden."

Lovely.

"Copy that, Control. Zero-One, out." Dawson turned to the others who were in the process of gearing up. "Well, boys, this is another Charlie-Foxtrot."

Niner looked at him. "What now?"

"No weapons."

"Bullshit."

"No bullshit. State says no weapons, and we can't gear up at the consulate either. No US government issued weapons or equipment."

Atlas' deep voice rumbled in protest. "How the hell do they expect us to fight?" He jerked a thumb at Niner. "With his rapier wit?"

Niner's head bobbed, a finger jabbing the air between them. "Good one, cuz a rapier is a type of sword."

Atlas winked at him as he rose. "Exactly. And"—the big man stepped over and picked Niner up under the armpits, holding him out in front of him—"he doubles as a shield too."

Niner's foot made contact with Atlas' balls, the big man doubling over, dropping his much smaller counterpart. "I deserved that," he winced.

"Yes, you did." Niner patted him on the back. "And well done, I felt those through my boot. That's something to be proud of."

Jimmy shook his head. "And you wonder why there's confusion."

Niner whirled at his best friend. "Hey, I thought we settled all that?"

Jimmy shrugged. "The committee is in recess." He turned to Dawson. "So what are we going to do?"

Leather stepped forward, pushing a phone back into his pocket. "I've just called one of my contacts. He's going to meet us and equip us as best he can. No guns, but body armor, survival equipment, knives, that type of thing."

Dawson's head bobbed in approval. "That's a good start. Time is of the essence. We need to find our people before the hostiles decide they're not worth keeping around. And you can bet we're going to have local interference."

Leather smiled. "Not a problem. My guy says he can take care of that too."

Dawson grinned. "Glad we decided to pick you up." He pointed at Niner. "If the Colonel's man delivers, you give him a big kiss from all of us."

Everyone roared with laughter.

Except Niner.

O. R. Tambo International Airport
Gauteng, South Africa

Hugh Reading stretched his aching muscles as he cleared customs, his Interpol ID allowing him to use the diplomatic line. He looked back for the young woman he had shared a seat with and spotted her in a long line. She waved, a hopeful look on her face, probably wanting him to help expedite her departure, but he wasn't here to play the old fool.

An unfamiliar face approached, an ID flashed, ending any fantasies that might have been playing out in the back of his mind.

"Agent Hugh Reading?"

"Yes?"

The man smiled, sticking out a hand. "Agent Ndlovu, State Security Agency. I'm to be your liaison while you're here."

Reading's eyes narrowed as he shook the man's hand. "I wasn't expecting an escort."

The man grabbed Reading's bag. "Your office called."

"Huh. And here I thought I was on vacation."

Ndlovu smiled. "The situation has been explained to me. Your supervisor said to tell you he looks forward to your retirement."

Reading chuckled. His boss was an asshole, but his kind of asshole, so they got along just fine, as long as he wasn't getting in Reading's way. "It'll be a bloody cold day in hell before that happens." A sharp pain shot up his leg then spine, taking the breath out of him. He winced.

Though my body might be on a different schedule.

"I understand. It's hard to give up a job one loves." He held out his hand. "This way. I've arranged another flight for you."

"Another?"

"Where your friends are located is over five hours from here by car. If we fly, we'll be there in about an hour."

Reading resisted groaning at the prospect of another hour on an airplane, though anything would be better than five hours in a car. "So, what can you tell me?"

Ndlovu shook his head. "Not much, I'm afraid. Local police arrived on the accident scene a few hours ago."

"What did they find?"

"Two bodies."

Reading tensed. "Have they been identified?"

"One was their guide from the resort, the other a young white boy, probably American if their State Department is to be believed."

Reading breathed a sigh of relief it not his friends. "Have they begun a search?"

Ndlovu shook his head, pointing through a large set of windows at the breaking sun. "Not yet. They said it wasn't safe until dawn. They should be starting shortly."

Reading stopped, Ndlovu turning to face him. "Are you having me on? They haven't been looking?"

"This is Africa, Agent Reading. It's not safe to be roaming it at night."

Reading glared at him. "My friends are out there roaming it right now."

"Yes, and let us hope they survived the night. We'll find them today if they're alive."

Reading frowned, not liking the condition put on the success of his mission. "I'd like to get to the scene as soon as we get there."

"The guide has a brother who is involved in poaching. My briefing indicates your friend thought it was poachers chasing them. Rather than waste our time at the scene of the accident, I suggest we start at the brother's home."

Reading agreed it was a good idea. The locals could search better than he could. If he could find out where this brother might be hiding, it could give the search team somewhere to look. "Good. When's our flight?"

Ndlovu tapped his watch. "Right now. They're holding the plane for us."

Andrew Street, Nelspruit, South Africa

Dawson stepped out of the rear door of the store, long shadows cast by the rising sun still concealing them slightly. He climbed into the back of a waiting SUV with the others, Leather's contact true to his word. With the last door shut, they pulled away quickly, though quietly.

Leather shook the driver's hand from the passenger seat. "I'd make introductions, but I can't remember what colors of the palette they're posing as today."

His contact laughed. "Well, I'm Frik. Pleased to meet you, gentlemen. That little cut-through you guys just did should leave your tail wondering what happened to you, and by the time they figure out where you went, you'll already be in the park." He jabbed a thumb over his shoulder. "Back there we have your standard issue survival gear for a visit to the park. In a hidden panel underneath your seats, there're knives and body armor and a few other tricks. I couldn't get guns on such short notice since the Colonel here insists we keep things all legal-like."

"No worries, we'll forage what we need." Dawson started hauling the supplies forward, passing the backpacks out, each man beginning an inventory.

Frik glanced in his mirror. "Where do you think you'll find guns?"

Niner grinned. "On the bodies of the dead."

Frik's head bobbed as if he weren't shocked by anything.

Dawson put the backpack at his feet. "How far are we?"

"If your CIA is right, we're about ninety minutes from their last known location. You're lucky. We're farther than that from the lodge, but the route they took is a double-back. We should hopefully get pretty close before they even start moving." He pointed at the sun, a sliver of it visible. "If we're lucky, they're not even awake yet."

Niner peered out the window. "Killing them in their sleep would be nice."

Dawson checked his watch. "I don't think we'll get that lucky."

Near Poacher's Camp

Greater Kruger National Park, South Africa

Acton's heart slammed as he lay prone on the hilltop, peering toward the camp about half a mile away. Everyone was awake now, equipment being loaded into vehicles, the hostages, including Laura, shoved into the back of one. The ringleader shouted something and Laura was hauled out and put into the back of another vehicle, one that turned out to be Tladi's.

He's singled her out. Why?

His imagination suggested possibilities he didn't want to contemplate.

The engines roared to life and they pulled out, promptly executing U-turns that had them heading back the way they came. Acton cursed, scrambling back down the hill, there only one reason they'd do that—they were coming this way. They had probably used the hill as a blind against anyone searching for them, as he had used it against them.

Or they had figured out where the mine was, and it was on this side of the hill.

The idea had the archaeologist in him excited.

Though that wasn't who he was today.

Yet whatever the reason, it meant they would soon be discovered.

He hit the ground, grabbing the already packed gear. "We've gotta go, now!"

Courtney's eyes widened as she looked about. "What's wrong?"

Acton grabbed her, sprinting in the opposite direction the poachers would be coming from. "They reversed course. I think they're going to round the hill and come this way." He glanced at Courtney as she slowed down slightly, tugging her along. Her eyes were wide with fear.

"We've gotta hide!"

"Yes, but we've also got some time. Let's cover as much distance as we can. Remember, we need to track them."

She stopped resisting, running beside him. "I don't think we're going to get that lucky again."

She was right, though there was one thing in their favor. The destination of these men wasn't outside of the park, it was an abandoned mine somewhere in the area. If they were lucky, it wasn't far, and the fact he had seen lights in the distance last night told him they were near the edge of the park, so the mine had to be somewhere close.

Come on, God, give us one more lucky break!

Skukuza Airport, South Africa

Reading regarded himself in the mirror, satisfied. He had been traveling for over half a day and was exhausted, though anxious to get underway, Ndlovu busy requisitioning a vehicle. He had spent the delay washing up and changing clothes, the ten minutes time well spent.

Presentable again.

Ndlovu poked his head into the bathroom. "Ready?"

"Yes. Did you get a vehicle?"

"Yes, though the choices were limited."

"A ride is a ride." Reading stepped out of the bathroom and into the hallway, Ndlovu standing with two insulated cups. "What's this?"

"Coffee for me, tea for you."

Reading smiled, taking the cup. "How'd you know?"

"You're a Brit, aren't you?"

Reading chuckled, taking a sip as they headed from the small terminal, hiding his wince. It wasn't very good, but it would do. "How far away are we?"

"Less than an hour."

"Then let's move. My friends might not have that long."

They stepped outside and Ndlovu walked over to a ridiculously small Ford Fiesta. Reading said nothing, there no time for complaints, instead tossing his carry-on into the back seat and climbing into the passenger side. His knees pressed against the dash. "Not exactly built for comfort."

Ndlovu glanced at him sheepishly, the much shorter man with plenty of room. "Sorry, when you're barely 170 centimeters, legroom isn't exactly a consideration." He eyed Reading's situation. "Um, I can try to get us another vehicle."

Reading shook his head. "No, that'll just waste time. Let's go."

The car whined from the parking lot, the pickup next to nothing, his stabbing pain returning with each jolt of a pothole.

Bloody hell!

Operations Center 3, CIA Headquarters
Langley, Virginia

"If they don't find a place to hide soon, they're going to find them."

Leroux nodded, Child's assessment accurate and obvious. The drone was high enough for them to have footage of who they were assuming were the two professors, as well as three rapidly approaching vehicles driven by the hostiles. He glanced at Tong. "Where's Delta?"

"Entering the park now. If we knew where they were heading, we could save a lot of time."

Leroux agreed. In the Interpol agent's notes to Kane, he had mentioned the Kruger Gold. Reading up on what his staff had found out about it, it was a possibly massive stash of gold, and if they had indeed located it, he found it impossible to believe they'd simply be returning to their lodge to continue their vacation.

So that meant they hadn't found it.

But his gut was telling him they had found a clue as to where it was hidden, which could be what was keeping them alive.

"They're going for the gold," he said, stepping closer to the display. "They didn't have it with them, otherwise they would have killed them all and taken it. That means they either know where it is, or the hostiles *think* they know."

"That makes sense," agreed Child. "So wherever they're heading must be where it's hidden."

"Possibly, or the hostages have managed to make them think that's where it's hidden. Either way, once they get there, they're not going to need the hostages anymore." He frowned, tapping his chin. "If we knew where they were going, we could send Delta there directly." He turned to Child. "What do we know about the area? Anything that might fit the bill for a hiding place for a horde of gold?"

Child's fingers tapped away, an old map appearing. "We found this. There're several abandoned mines in the area." A red dot appeared. "This is the closest. My bet is they're going there."

"What makes you think that?"

"Umm, it's the only one on that side of the hill?"

Leroux smiled. "Who's got the legendary gut now?" He turned to Tong. "Reroute Delta to that location, they might be able to actually gain some time."

Greater Kruger National Park, South Africa

Acton glanced over his shoulder, still seeing nothing. They were making good time for being on foot, but there was no way to compete with vehicles designed for the terrain. The only good thing was that the ground was fairly rough, which would slow them down.

He just prayed they were coming in this direction and he wasn't leading them farther away.

Gears gnashed behind them and he looked, the first vehicle, obscured by dust, emerged from around a bend in the hillside. He grabbed Courtney by the hand, spotting an outcropping nearby. "Come on! Over here!"

He raced toward the small bit of cover, only a few feet deep, and pushed her into the rock face, Courtney's chest heaving with fear against his as the noise of the vehicles grew.

"What if they see us?"

"Then we surrender. No heroics. Nobody gets shot today."

She buried her head in his shoulder, squeezing her eyes shut as the vehicles blasted by, the dry ground creating a cloud of dust around them, obscuring the occupants' view of the surrounding area, especially of that behind them.

And then they were out of sight.

Acton stepped out, staring after them, there no way they could spot them through the dust. He glanced behind to make sure there wasn't a straggler vehicle, though he knew there wasn't, having counted three vehicles passing them.

He grabbed Courtney by the hand, urging her forward as he sprinted after them. "Let's go!" As they raced after the small caravan carrying a dozen armed men and his wife, he prayed wherever they were going wasn't far.

And that when they arrived there, the hostages, his wife, wouldn't be summarily executed.

Abandoned Mine

Greater Kruger National Park, South Africa

"There it is, boss."

Laura looked to where the former miner pointed, and spotted a cluster of brush, about twenty feet from the ground. She stared for a moment, not sure what she was seeing, when suddenly she discerned an opening behind the bushes.

Tladi groaned. "What the hell is it doing up there?"

The miner shrugged. "Dunno. Didn't dig it."

Tladi frowned as they pulled to a halt, his driver turning the vehicle to face the open ground, the others doing the same, Laura now convinced it was a habit they had developed to allow a quicker getaway should police or park rangers arrive. She glanced back in the direction they had come, wondering where James was. They hadn't traveled far, barely a couple of miles from where she estimated he might have been. If he had survived the night, they probably drove right past him.

Then a thought occurred to her that gave her a glimmer of hope.

If he hadn't survived, surely they would have seen his body?

She frowned.

Not if whatever had killed him had dragged him away.

The hope was gone.

Though she still had her faith in him, in that she'd know if he were dead.

And she knew he wasn't.

He was still out there, doing everything he could to save her and the others.

Because that's who he was.

And it was that desperation, that determination, that had her concerned. Part of her wanted him to find her, but another part wanted him to stay away. He was one man against a dozen. He was hopelessly outnumbered and outgunned. What could he possibly do to save them without getting killed?

Tladi grabbed her arm, pulling her out of the vehicle. "Okay, expert lady, you lead the way."

She yanked her arm free, concealing the pain she was in from his iron grip. She scanned the area for a way to access the entrance, spotting a thin pathway winding up the hill in a series of switchbacks. She pointed. "There." She headed for the path, everyone else forming a line behind her, and soon reached the entrance. Two of Tladi's men squeezed past her, hacking the bushes away with machetes, the boarded-up entrance soon clearly visible for all to see. The boards were kicked, the dry wood splitting easily, the poachers pulling them away and tossing them to the ground below.

She held out a hand. "Flashlight."

Tladi gestured to one of his men who slapped one in her hand, none too gently. She resisted the urge to wince, instead smiling.

"Thank you." She flicked it on and stepped inside.

Tladi grabbed her by the arm, whipping her around, shining the flashlight on his face so she could see his sincerity. "Find me my gold, or die."

Laura ignored him, instead yanking her arm free once more before moving deeper into the mine, the timbers rotted, signs of cave-ins of varying ages evident. And there were animal tracks, something that sent her heart pounding slightly harder than it already was, though it was difficult to tell how fresh they were.

Yet her biggest fear wasn't surprising an animal that might have made this their den.

It was that they might find the gold.

And their captors would no longer need them alive.

Approaching Abandoned Mine
Greater Kruger National Park, South Africa

Acton, exhausted, pushed forward, his heart hammering, his legs burning. He normally had no problem running, going for five mile runs all the time, even running marathons in his youth, but it was different in hiking boots, hungry, thirsty, over uneven terrain, carrying a rifle, and doing it at an all-out, desperate sprint.

Courtney grabbed his arm, dragging him to a halt.

He doubled over, hands on his knees, gasping. "What?"

She pointed. "Isn't that them?"

He turned his head to see, still bent over, and would have breathed a sigh of relief if he could.

Three vehicles, lined up against the hillside, positioned for a quick getaway.

Thank God! Finally, something goes right!

Acton stepped back toward the hillside and out of sight, Courtney getting the canteen out of the backpack, finally showing signs of fatigue. She handed it to him and he poured a cup, downing it, before drinking a second more slowly. "Thanks."

Courtney risked a peek toward the vehicles, immediately pressing back against the rock. "What now? There's like a dozen of them and only two of us."

She was right. They needed the cavalry to arrive now, but he had no idea if they were even on their way. Reading would be doing everything he could, rescue would *eventually* arrive, yet beyond that, he had no idea what was going on outside their little cone of reality.

That meant he couldn't wait.

If they had indeed found the mine, then the gold was likely inside, about to be discovered. And as soon as that happened, there'd be no need to keep Laura and the others alive. In fact, he was surprised they hadn't killed the others already, though Laura had probably made some sort of deal for her cooperation.

Cooperation that might no longer be needed in a matter of minutes.

He had to take action, do something, even if it might mean his death.

He looked about, nobody evident at first, then froze, spotting two guards about twenty feet above the ground, at the entrance of what must be the mine Sipho had spoken of. It was an odd place for an entrance, definitely not convenient for moving any ore that might have been found.

He put a finger to his lips, taking Courtney's hand and placing it over her mouth, then pointed at the two men guarding the entrance. Her eyes bulged, but she kept quiet, removing her hand.

"What do we do now?"

"There has to be another entrance. We need to find it."

Courtney's eyes narrowed. "What makes you think that?"

"Because no one puts the entrance to a mine twenty feet above the ground. That's probably for air or for dumping whatever they were mining out to the ground below. There has to be a ground level entrance around here, close by."

"But how are we going to find it?"

"Well, we didn't pass it, so it must be farther on. Just stay here, I'll go find it." He turned to go when she grabbed his arm.

"We stick together."

He frowned, there no arguing with her. "Fine, stick to my six—"

"Huh?"

"Ass."

"Oh."

"—keep quiet, and stay as close to the hillside as you can. They don't have the angle to be able to see us from up there."

She nodded and Acton poked his head out, watching the men above. If he could see them, then they could see him, at least here. They had to clear about thirty feet to be under them, then the hillside took a bend where they would be unseen.

Both guards stepped into the mine, out of sight.

Acton grabbed Courtney's hand and sprinted across the gap, taking advantage of the lapse in security, all the while his head tilted up, eyes glued to the entrance.

He spotted movement.

And they pulled up, pressing against the wall, voices overhead, calm, they evidently not having been spotted.

He held a finger to his lips, once again reminding Courtney of their predicament, then slowly slithered along the rock face, toward the bend, his eyes on where the poachers might look should they lean over for some reason.

Courtney sneezed.

Like a sound!

He grabbed her hand, yanking her the rest of the distance and around the bend, slapping his own hand over her mouth, his pounding heart overwhelming his senses as he tried to hear if they had been discovered.

Nothing.

"Sorry!" she whispered.

He pointed for her to keep going, and they walked for a few hundred feet before Acton spotted what he was searching for. Another entrance, clearly manmade, in the hillside.

At ground level.

Courtney smiled, apparently impressed. "You were right!"

"It's been known to happen." He pointed at a stand of trees nearby. "I want you to stay over there, out of sight, while I go inside."

"No way. We stick together."

Acton shook his head, there no arguing this time. "No, it's going to be too dangerous. I have to go inside, alone." He jabbed a finger at the trees. "Over there, now."

"But you'll be killed!"

"It's my wife. I have to try and save her."

"You're crazy!"

He handed her the gun, perhaps proving her point. "Take it."

"Won't you need it?"

He shook his head, drawing the knife from her belt. "This will be more useful in there."

Abandoned Mine

Greater Kruger National Park, South Africa

Tladi followed the white woman, their progress excruciatingly slow. She examined every beam, every brace, every part of every wall, even the animal prints in the dirt.

And it was tasking his patience.

Yet every time he challenged her on it, she had an explanation, a perfectly reasonable explanation.

And it was infuriating.

He hated people who thought they were smarter than him.

And he really hated people who actually were.

Yet this was taking forever, and by now people were searching for them, rich white tourists disappearing sure to attract plenty of attention. They didn't have a lot of time before the area would be swarming with police and rangers, and if they put a helicopter in the air, there might be no avoiding detection. Their only hope was to find the gold, kill the hostages, dump their bodies somewhere away from the discovery, then lay low in town until they could come back for it.

They'll come straight to you.

With his brother dead, they'd definitely pay him a visit. But so what? No one could expect that he'd kill his own brother. And besides, his wife would give him an alibi, as she always did, and he'd play the grieving family member, crying about how he'd have to go tell their poor mother, and then they'd move on.

I'll have to move the stash!

It was stupid to store it on his property, yet he had no choice—he didn't trust any of the others. He had a buyer from China coming next week, then it would all be gone, but now, with the prospect of the gold, he would have to take the stash and hide it somewhere, even if it meant abandoning it.

Nothing could trace back to him.

He was about to have millions, all to himself.

They came to a junction, three more tunnels extending out from the one they were currently in. "Which one?"

The woman turned toward him. "No way to know. We'll start with the one on the left, and if we don't find anything, come back here and continue with the next."

Tladi's chest tightened in frustration. "I thought you were an expert?"

"I am. And this is the way it's done."

He growled. "To hell with that." He pointed to the shaft in the middle then looked at his men. "You two, down that one, you two the one on the right, you with me. The rest stay with the hostages." He shoved the woman into the tunnel on the left. "Let's hurry this up!"

Above Abandoned Mine

Greater Kruger National Park, South Africa

Niner and Dawson peered over the edge of the cliff at the two hostiles below, guarding what Langley thought was the entrance to a mine, a mine that might have enough gold stashed in it for them all to retire comfortably. Control had wisely rerouted them along a path from where they couldn't be spotted, costing them barely ten minutes, their vehicles parked only a klick from the hostiles'.

Dawson crept back from the edge, Niner following, Dawson briefing the others. "Two hostiles, forty feet below our position."

Atlas dropped two bundles of rope at their feet, Leather's contact having supplied them well. "These should be long enough."

Niner eyed him. "Should?"

Atlas shrugged, tossing him a harness then climbing into his own. "I'll go with you in case you're scared I'm wrong."

Niner prepped for the descent as Dawson cut off any retort, continuing with the briefing.

"There're three vehicles below, no guards, so the rest must be inside, including the hostages." He turned to Niner and Atlas, already prepped. "Get down, kill them quick and silent, and don't dump the bodies over the edge. We want their weapons."

"Roger that," said Niner, turning to Atlas with a grin. "Race you?"

Atlas gave him a look. "Little man, gravity dictates I win."

"Fleet of foot says I do." He approached the edge, Jimmy and Dawson holding his rope, Leather and his man holding Atlas'. He glanced at them. "You'll be wishing you were on my rope in a second."

He stepped over, running down the side of the cliff as if it were a Sunday morning jog at Bragg, his knife at the ready as he picked where he'd put his feet on each step to minimize the loosening of any debris, not wanting to warn the rapidly nearing hostiles of their impending doom.

He pushed off slightly from the cliff, flipping forward, letting those above feed out the rope at the pace he had set, as he dove headfirst toward his target, the big man right at his side. He reached out with his left hand, gripping his target's face from behind and buried six inches of his blade into the side of the man's neck. Giving it a twist, he silenced him before touching the ground.

He glanced over at Atlas with an 'I win' look.

Atlas shook his head, tapping his chest with his bloody knife, his hand clasped over his struggling target's mouth.

He broke the man's neck, Niner frowning as his still bled out.

He wins.

Niner pulled his man to the side of the entrance and listened, hearing nothing from inside, their attendance at the party not yet discovered. Niner took the beat-up AK-47 that had been slung over his guy's shoulder, it a reasonable score. He pulled the mag and cursed.

One round.

He looked at Atlas, his guy packing an old revolver. Atlas flicked it open.

One round.

What is this, a theme?

Abandoned Mine

Greater Kruger National Park, South Africa

What the hell are you doing?

Acton knew he was an idiot for entering the mine alone, yet what choice did he have? It was Laura, his wife, the love of his life, the woman who had saved his life before, and who would without hesitation sacrifice her own to save it again.

As would he.

Though sacrificing to save the one you loved was noble, it was foolish if it was merely sacrificing oneself.

If there was no hope in saving the person, the sacrifice meant little.

If life were a math equation.

But it wasn't.

Trying to save her was the right thing to do.

He just had no clue how to do it with a knife in one hand and a flashlight in the other.

He could hear nothing ahead, only his own breathing, which for the moment suited him fine. Quiet was good, for surely the act of killing the hostages would be a noisy affair.

Unless the tunnel you're in doesn't connect to where they are.

It was possible, though he doubted it. These old shafts usually connected at some point, though through cave-ins, they could indeed be cut off now.

He frowned at the thought.

Yet pressed forward, the beam from the flashlight aimed at his feet to not only spot any hidden dangers, but to avoid it being seen by anyone who might be ahead. He had to hope they had no such worries, and that he'd spot their flashlights first.

His hand squeezed around the hilt of the knife, realizing that there would be no choice but to kill anyone he came upon, even the slightest noise or hesitation from him could reveal his presence, and perhaps seal the fate of the others.

Something echoed ahead.

And he froze.

Niner crept forward in the darkness, wishing he had a pair of night vision goggles. They had flashlights though couldn't risk being seen by those ahead, which meant relying on their other senses, mostly those fed by the holes in the side of their heads.

And one nice thing about bad guys who didn't know you were coming, was they were quite loud.

Like those just around a bend he could barely make out, there obviously some sort of light source ahead. He put his hand out behind him, pressing it against Jimmy's chest to have him hold, the silent signal passed back as Niner crept forward, choosing his steps carefully.

He found the source, a flashlight sitting on the floor, pointed up, providing barely enough light for him to pick out who needed to be killed and who didn't.

He stepped back, hand behind him, finding Jimmy where he left him. He put his mouth to the operator's ear, whispering his intel. "Six hostiles, four hostages. Hostages are on the floor against the right-hand wall, hostiles are spread out in front. We're short one hostage, so we need to do this quietly. I'm going to try and thin the herd."

Jimmy patted him on the back, acknowledging the message, turning to pass it on to the others. Niner knelt and picked up a small stone, tossing it against the other side of the wall.

Now for the fun part.

"Did you hear that?"

Jacob glanced at his cousin then back at the young woman, wondering if Tladi was serious about a party with them after this was all done. He could tell that he'd be into it by how things down below were reacting to the thought. "No."

"Well, I heard something."

"You're always hearing things."

"No, I swear."

"It's your imagination. Next thing you'll be saying there's ghosts."

His cousin raised his weapon, turning toward the entrance tunnel. "I'm checking it out."

"Go ahead if you're so sure."

"You're not coming with me?"

Jacob grunted. "I'm not chasing ghosts."

"You afraid?"

"I ain't afraid of no ghosts."

His cousin chuckled, Jacob's eyes narrowing as he stared at him, replaying what he had just said, a smile breaking out as everyone started to laugh.

"So are you coming?"

Jacob shook his head. "Like I said, I didn't hear anything. You check it out."

"You *are* afraid."

Jacob ignored him.

"Fine." His cousin stepped away from the light, flicking on his flashlight as he headed back toward the entrance.

Fool.

Niner pressed against the wall, his knife ready as his finely tuned hearing picked up the tentative, cautious steps of a hostile coming their way, laughter petering out around the bend. It would have to be quick and silent, otherwise they'd be overwhelmed with five more armed poachers, odds that could get tricky in these tight quarters.

The beam from a flashlight sliced through the ink-black, illuminating the opposite wall, the man stepping into view. Niner waited, his breathing controlled as he kept his heart rate steady, letting the adrenaline flow smoothly to give him heightened reflexes, but not too hot to cause mistakes.

He reached out, clamping a hand over the man's mouth as he slit his throat with the other. Jimmy stepped forward, grabbing the man's hand with the flashlight before it could fall, Niner silently lowering the dead man to the ground.

One down, five to go.

Acton inched his way deeper, the shaft he was in coming to a three-way split, this his fear, and why he had made it a point to drag his foot on the dirt floor every few feet. He didn't care if anyone spotted his trail, there no way of knowing if it were made today or ten years ago. All he cared about was not getting hopelessly lost inside a system he was certain had no logical layout.

Two flashlight beams appeared ahead, approaching slowly, two men talking, their voices echoing off the walls, clear they thought they were alone. He wished he could understand the language so he might glean some information from them, but he didn't, though from the tone he had the impression they were complaining about something. He stepped into the shadows, pressing behind a support beam as the two men continued past, down a shaft he thankfully hadn't just come from, they liable to find Courtney if they did.

He watched as they played their beams along the walls and ceiling, clearly searching for something, and smiled, spotting in their light what appeared to be a severely rotted timber.

And a pickaxe handle on the ground underneath.

He edged forward, picking up the handle as the two men disappeared around a bend, then flicked his flashlight back on, examining the ceiling. He tapped at it with the handle, dirt crumbling down.

Do I risk it?

One of the men said something, the utterance sounding like frustration, the footfalls approaching again, this time quicker.

Dead end?

The beams of light reappeared and he cursed.

No choice.

He swung the axe handle, shattering the rotted beam, the noise deafening in the enclosed space.

And nothing happened.

Oh shit!

Excited exclamations from the two men were followed by heavy footfalls.

He swung again.

And again.

And again.

Then all hell broke loose.

Tladi froze, a rumbling sound coming from somewhere in the distance getting louder. His heart hammered and he glanced up at the ceiling, appearing sound for the moment.

"What was that?"

The woman shrugged. "Probably a cave-in. I told you that you needed to be an expert to deal with these types of situations. You refused to listen."

Tladi felt a rage build in his stomach, sick of the attitude from this privileged white woman, her constant superior tone, her constant disrespect, almost enough to make him kill her right now, regardless of whether they found the gold.

No reward is worth this!

He jammed the barrel of his gun into her stomach. "If my men are dead, then so are you."

She glared at him. "Your men are *certainly* dead, and it's *because* of you." She shrugged. "Besides, who cares? It just means there're fewer people for you to share the gold with."

Tladi relaxed the weapon slightly, the woman having a point.

He turned to his man, who thankfully didn't understand English. "Go check it out."

"Yes, boss."

"What the hell was that?"

Jacob was on his feet, there no ignoring the massive rumbling sound as it approached, a cloud of dust rolling over them before the sound, and debris, settled. But he knew what it was, a sound that terrified anyone who had worked in the mines.

Cave-in.

He looked at the others. "Maybe we should check it out."

His other cousin shook his head. "To hell with that, I'm staying right here."

"Coward. Those are our brothers. I'm going."

"Fine, fine, I'll go."

Jacob turned to the others, nodding toward the exit tunnel. "See if he found any ghosts."

Niner smiled as he watched two of the men leave, the others chuckling over something that was said. One of them approached his position, flashlight stretched far ahead of him, much more cautious than his compatriot who lay beside Jimmy, exsanguinated. The hostile carefully played his light over the walls, ceiling, and floor, as if he expected something to jump out at him from any direction.

Not good.

Niner pressed against the wall but knew he'd be spotted this time.

He'd have to time it perfectly.

The flashlight came around the corner, catching his knee then moving on for a moment before flicking back.

Busted.

Something was yelled.

Niner stepped out, yanking the man forward then past him, sending him toward Jimmy to take care of. A grunt and gasp behind him told him business was good as he surged toward the two remaining hostiles. He plunged his knife into the stomach of the first startled man, clamping a hand over his mouth as he twisted the blade, then pulling it free, his entire body already spinning toward the final hostile, he buried the blade deep into the other's skull, silencing him instantly.

Scrambled-eggs-for-brains collapsed as his friend bled out, Niner still holding him as the death throes finished their final act, the small intersection of tunnels filling with flashlights as the rest of his team entered.

"United States Soldiers," whispered Dawson. "Remain quiet!"

Murmurs of relief filled the tiny area when a shot rang out from the darkness, Leather dropping. Niner spun toward the sound, his knife loosed, burying into the chest of the surprise newcomer.

Though not before revealing their position with an agonizing cry.

They had been discovered.

"What was that?"

Laura had already spun toward the sound, there no point in playing stupid. Instead, she decided keeping her mouth shut was the best option. Someone had fired a weapon. A single shot. It could have been an accident, though someone had cried out, and it sounded like one of fear, of pain.

Tladi didn't wait for an answer. "We need to find another way out of here." He grabbed her by the arm, squeezing tight, and led her deeper into the tunnel. She resisted, charging foolishly into a century-old abandoned mine idiotic. "Let's go!"

"No, you'll get us both killed!"

He jabbed the gun into her ribs. "Move or you're dead." She glared at him but realized she had no choice. Whatever had happened had Tladi scared, which could only be good for her.

Should she survive his panicked reaction.

Could help have arrived?

"Fine." She continued forward. As she played her flashlight out in front of them, no longer searching for the lost gold but merely attempting self-preservation, she dismissed the idea.

Surely help would be much louder than a single shot and a lone shout.

She felt a queasiness almost overwhelm her.

Unless that single shot was someone shooting James!

She slowed slightly, a shove to her back sending her stumbling forward again as she replayed the cry in her mind.

Could it have been him?

She had no way of knowing, no possible way, yet within moments she was convinced it had indeed been him.

And he was dead.

Acton breathed a sigh of relief as the two new men that had been approaching him spun toward the sound of the gunshot. They sprinted back toward where they had come, which had to be where the hostages, and Laura, were.

And a horrifying thought occurred to him.

They're shooting them!

His heart slammed against his ribcage as he resisted the urge to rush after them, instead carefully moving forward, it far too easy to stumble upon someone, or something, that could mean his certain death.

Tladi slapped his hand over Laura's mouth as they came out of a bend in the shaft, it splitting into three. He yanked her against the wall and into the shadows, pressing the gun against her head. Someone was coming, a diffused beam from a flashlight visible to their left for a brief moment before they were buried in shadows, whoever it was, creeping along toward them.

It couldn't have been one of Tladi's men, though perhaps it was, the gunshot potentially putting even these murderers on edge. But if they suspected the shot wasn't from one of their own, then who did they think it was?

It was the silence that was killing her.

A single shot, a single cry, then nothing.

If they had shot James or one of the others, surely there would have been some shouting, surely someone would have been sent to find Tladi, but no one had come.

It made no sense.

Suddenly the light was visible, then the shadow of the figure, his hand held in front of the beam, giving him enough light to see his way, though not enough to reveal his position to those who might be around the next bend.

And reflecting just enough of his silhouette that she knew instantly who it was, his form seared on her mind forever.

James!

"Is one of you Courtney Tasker?"

Silence, then the young woman spoke. "She ran away. I think she's safe."

Dawson sliced the ropes binding them as Leather was helped to his feet. Dawson glanced over his shoulder at him. "You good?"

"Just my pride wounded. That bastard came out of nowhere."

Niner shrugged. "Don't look at me." He pointed at the tunnel where the man had emerged from. "I consider that Sword. These two are Omaha and Utah. That was clearly a British tunnel."

Dawson chuckled as he helped the hostages up. He pointed to Jimmy. "Get them outside. Signal control that we have not recovered the Secretary's daughter." He flicked his flashlight at Leather and his man. "Go with them." He turned to the others. "Where's Laura Palmer?"

The older black man replied. "He took her." He pointed down Sword. "Down there."

Dawson turned back to Jimmy. "Tell Control we think the other person with Acton is Tasker, not Palmer."

"Roger that." Jimmy led the hostages to safety, Leather and his man following them out.

Dawson looked at Atlas and Niner. "Three tunnels, three of us. Shall we?"

Niner smiled, stepping into Omaha. "See you on the other side."

Belfast, South Africa

Reading shook his head, his discomfort from being wedged into the tiny vehicle forgotten as he witnessed true suffering around him. He had never seen real poverty before, not in person, not in a modern country.

This was unbelievable.

In the jungles of the Amazon, where the primitive tribes existed, he had experienced firsthand their simple, basic lives, lives that were rich in a way Western civilization could never hope to comprehend.

Happiness, contentedness, was its own wealth.

Kinti and her family were happy with their lives the way they were.

Simple. Pure. One with nature, with the jungle.

Sometimes ignorance is bliss.

If you don't know what it is like to be "rich" by Western standards, then you're never miserable because your life doesn't compare. How can you be upset because you don't have a big television, when you don't even know what one is, when you can't even conceptualize a computer, a tablet or a phone, a meal served at a fine restaurant, or a car to show off to your neighbors?

When everyone is living the same way you are, and you've never seen or even heard of something different, envy and jealousy over material possessions never enter the equation.

But here, everyone living in the squalor that surrounded him, knew there was a better life, a better way, and it meant they were fully aware of how horrible their lives actually were.

It was heartbreaking.

Having just seen the wealth and modernity of Johannesburg, then less than two hours later to be in the same country, experiencing the ramshackle homes that lined the dirt roads, tucked away so the pampered heading to the luxury resorts only miles away wouldn't feel uncomfortable, he was flabbergasted.

He looked at Ndlovu. "How do people live like this?"

Ndlovu glanced at him. "You in the West I think forget how most of the world lives, especially in societies where significant minorities have westernized."

Reading's head bobbed slowly as they drove through the town. "Like Brazil." He had seen it when Jim and Laura had treated him to World Cup tickets, but they had been inside the bubble of the event, not seeing the poverty, instead seeing what the Brazilian government had wanted them to see.

Much like the Olympics.

Ndlovu flicked his wrist at their surroundings. "Exactly like Brazil. Rich enough to host Olympic games, but too poor to provide basic services to their population—unless they're rich." He sighed. "In South Africa, it is two different worlds. The white world, and those like me who have been able to live in it, then this, this disgrace." He shook his head, his voice lowering. "I was born into this, but was lucky. My father worked for the ANC and was able to get a good job when apartheid was abolished. He was able to get me an education, to lift us out of this." He shook his head. "But there are only so many jobs." He pointed to a house ahead. "According to what we were told at the store, this is it."

They pulled up beside the humble home, Reading following Ndlovu to the door, looking about with unease, painfully aware he was the only white man in the entire neighborhood, and that all eyes were on him.

Now I know how a minority must feel back home.

Ndlovu rapped on the door, it rattling noisily. The door opened moments later, a colorfully dressed woman answering with a smile until she saw him.

Still no trust?

A brief exchange in their native tongue occurred before she regarded Reading warily, fear in her widened eyes. "Yes, I speak English."

"Wonderful, that will make things much easier for my friend. As I said, I'm Agent Ndlovu, State Security Agency, and this is Agent Reading, Interpol."

Reading extended a hand. "Ma'am."

She took it, her handshake weak and brief.

Ndlovu continued. "We're looking for Tladi Tsabalala. Is he here?"

She frowned, the fear gone, derision replacing it as she snapped out an annoyed shake of the head. "No."

"Do you know where he is?"

"I never ask."

"When did you last see him?"

She pursed her lips for a moment. "Yesterday."

"Do you mind if we look around?"

She shrugged. "I got nothin' to hide." She stepped aside and Ndlovu entered, Reading following him into the house in name only, though it was clearly a home, those who lived here doing so with as much dignity as their circumstances allowed, it clean and tidy, with several personal items decorating the walls and shelves.

Reading was about to compliment her when he bit his tongue, realizing it might come off as condescending. They pressed deeper inside, finding several children in a back room surrounding a single schoolbook, then a rear door that opened into a dusty yard containing a shed slapped together from scrap corrugated metal.

"What's in there?" asked Ndlovu.

The fear in the woman's eyes returned.

"Well?"

She shrugged. "I-I don't know."

Ndlovu looked about, his eyes settling on an axe nearby. He picked it up, breaking off the padlock holding the door in place, Reading pretty certain a simple shove would have brought the entire affair to the ground.

Ndlovu tossed the axe aside, pulling open the door.

Reading gasped.

The stench was overwhelming, rolling out like a liquid, Reading stepping aside and pulling a handkerchief from his pocket then pressing it against his mouth and nose.

"What the bloody hell is that?"

Ndlovu frowned, stepping inside. "Rotting flesh."

Reading followed as Ndlovu hauled a tarp off a pile in the back, then gasped at the both heartbreaking and infuriating sight. Dozens of elephant tusks and rhino horns were stacked against the back wall, representing the murder of scores of innocent creatures for no other reason than greed and East Asian erections.

Ndlovu shook his head. "Well, we've definitely got the right guy."

Reading stepped outside, gulping in several lungsful of air. He looked at the woman. "We need to know where he is."

"I d-don't know."

Ndlovu stepped outside, wagging a finger at her. "You're in a lot of trouble. Cooperate, and I might just leave you out of this."

She turned away, staring at her children pressed against the back door. Her shoulders slumped. "Last I saw him, he say he going to Florence's house."

Ndlovu exchanged a slight smile with Reading. "Why?"

"I-I don't know."

Abandoned Mine

Greater Kruger National Park, South Africa

Courtney made her way to the mine entrance, it taking too long. The professor was right—she should remain outside, though being alone was never a state she had taken to, triggering feelings of abandonment and isolation that far too easily sent her into states of depression, or apparently, in this new situation, panic.

A lifetime of nannies, drivers, maids and tutors had meant she barely had a minute alone.

That was why she surrounded herself with friends, no matter how tenuous the connection might be.

Like this trip.

She thought she loved Dyson, though if she were honest with herself, she didn't. He was her boy toy, someone to satisfy her carnal needs, someone to have on her arm when a plus-one was required, there a lot of that in her daddy's life even before he turned to politics.

He was a friend, she supposed, and she definitely had some sort of feelings for him. It had hurt when he was killed, but thoughts of never being with him again, or shattered future plans, had never crossed her mind.

Only how she'd be blamed for bringing him, and how she'd now have to find someone else and train them.

I really am awful!

And Gina and Phil were hardly friends. They hadn't even been the first she had invited on the trip. If she thought about it, she had invited half a dozen couples before finding someone to say yes. Her chest tightened slightly with a sudden realization. It wasn't that these people had been busy, it was that they didn't want to travel with her. Gina and Phil had agreed because they could never have afforded a trip like this on their own, and were probably willing to tolerate two weeks with her just to have the experience of a luxury safari vacation.

Oh my God! I've got no friends!

She thought back on her life, on her childhood, and how it was always playdates, arranged by her parents, the children under the watchful eye of a nanny while the adults discussed some charity or business venture, the playdates merely excuses to either pick her family's pockets, or they their guests.

She was a tool, used by her father to get what he wanted, or by others wanting something from him.

Does Daddy even love me?

Her eyes burned, then she shook away the thought, there no doubt in her mind he did. They spent plenty of time together when he wasn't busy, and even went on outings together, outings he had no need to go on, with no one joining them to monopolize his time.

No, he loved her.

At least she had that.

Even if she had no real friends.

I need to change.

But was it too late? She was a bitch, she knew it, though she had always thought that was one of the reasons people liked her. She'd treat those beneath her like shit, her friends would laugh, and they'd move on. Her money and name got them into all the best clubs, all the best parties, and invited to the exclusive sales with big name designers.

Money talked.

Though if she thought about it, her friends were merely using her as her daddy's friends used him. They wanted something from her. They wanted that access to the exclusive clubs, the hot parties, the amazing designers.

They weren't real friends at all.

They were leeches.

And she deserved it.

When she got home, she was pruning her friend list, no matter how painful it would be, even if it left her with no one on Facebook or Instagram.

She was going to learn from this.

Dyson was dead because of her arrogance, and if she had listened to the brave man now risking everything for the woman he loved, they never would have been driving that Jag, and they'd never have been involved in this situation.

Will anyone ever love me enough to risk their life?

She doubted it.

A noise from inside the mine had her heart in her throat, and feet scrambling to return her to her hiding place, but it was too far. She dove behind a large rock then peered out from behind it to see the bastard who had killed Dyson emerge, dragging the woman she had disrespected.

I've got to help her.

She stared at the gun, the debate raging. She was a good shot. An excellent shot, but with a weapon she was familiar with, surrounded by family or those she felt superior to, there no pressure beyond making her daddy proud.

Here she could miss and kill the woman.

She couldn't risk it.

Instead, she was forced to watch helplessly as he climbed into one of their vehicles and started it, peeling away from the mine and out of sight.

Now what do I do?

She gasped, remembering the guards that had been at the other entrance. Her head spun toward it as she realized she would now be in plain sight, then breathed a sigh of relief, they no longer there.

I wonder where they went.

She ducked as several men emerged from the mine entrance with her friends and the black couple.

Who are they?

She flattened onto the ground, out of sight, wishing the professor would return to tell her what to do.

Jimmy emerged into the sunlight, shielding his eyes for a moment, surveying the area for any hostiles, finding none. He paused. "Wait, weren't there three vehicles when we went in?"

Leather stepped toward the edge, peering down. "Yeah, somebody got away."

Jimmy shook his head. "Shit. And knowing our luck, they took Professor Palmer with them." He activated his comm. "Control, One-Zero. We've recovered four hostages. Gina Davidson and Phillip Thicke, plus the two South Africans. We believe the Secretary's daughter is with Professor Acton, over."

The reply was swift, and surprising. "One-Zero, Control. If that's the case, then she's about two hundred feet from your current location."

Jimmy's eyebrows popped as he searched the area, still coming up empty. "We're missing a vehicle out here. Are you sure she didn't leave in it?"

"Negative. One hostile left the area with who we now believe is Professor Palmer. We're looking at the target that was with Professor Acton right now. She's at your ten o'clock."

Jimmy did the mental math. "Are you saying there're no more hostages inside?"

"We still don't have a twenty on Professor Acton. We presume he's still inside, so watch your fire."

"Copy that." He turned to Leather's man. "Let them know Acton's still in there. Anyone else is hostile." Reese nodded, disappearing back inside as Jimmy began his way down the hillside, his eyes scanning the area where Control was certain their VIP was hiding.

He came to a stop, holding his arms out. "Courtney Tasker! I'm an American soldier sent here by your father to find you. Please come out."

Nothing.

And he didn't blame her, not after what she'd probably been through. He wasn't exactly in uniform, though he had to think he appeared less threatening than the poachers. He glanced at Leather, standing with the others.

Though he *doesn't look very friendly.*

"Ma'am, please reveal yourself. There's a drone overhead. We know exactly where you are. There's no danger."

Again nothing.

Then he remembered the briefing. "Your father said that his nickname for you is 'peaches'."

A burst of tanned blonde erupted from behind a rock, about fifty feet away, rushing toward him, her arms extended as tears flowed down her cheeks.

Shoulda started with that.

Courtney slammed into the soldier, wrapping her arms around him, her shoulders racked with sobs as the pressures of the past day finally overwhelmed her, the tenuous hold she had maintained over her emotions instantly gone as any responsibility she had to keep things together was now lifted.

They're American!

"Oh, thank God you're here!"

She felt the man pat her back, saying nothing, then she looked at the others as they descended the path carved into the cliff, reality demanding her attention once again. She pushed away, pointing toward the other entrance. "You have to help them! The professor, he's still inside! And they took his wife! I don't know where, but just a few minutes ago!"

The soldier nodded, smiling gently. "Yes, we know. We're tracking her now. And we'll find Professor Acton, don't worry."

Gina and Phil reached the ground and Courtney rushed toward them, hugging Gina hard as they all sobbed, Phil hugging them both, all the horrible things said, forgotten.

"Thank God you're both okay!" she cried.

"What are you doing here?" asked Gina. "We thought you got away."

"I came with the professor."

"That's insane! Why didn't you just wait for help?"

Courtney started to laugh, losing control. "He refused." Then she shook uncontrollably. "My God, he's *so* brave. He fought a lion!"

"What?"

"A lion! And so did I! I mean, I helped!" She lost all control as she looked at her friends. "I'm so sorry!" she cried.

Gina's forehead pressed against hers. "It's not your fault."

"No, it is. I'm so sorry for the way I treated you. For the way I treated everybody. I promise I'm going to be a better person. No more bitchy Courtney, I promise." She stared at Gina and Phil. "I really need friends right now. Real friends. Are we okay?"

Gina wrapped her arms around her, hugging her tight. "I'm looking forward to the new Courtney. She sounds great."

Courtney smiled, closing her eyes, and sobbed.

Niner stepped into the shadows, a single flashlight bouncing toward him. He knew it wasn't any of his team—they wouldn't be that stupid. But it could be the professor, though he couldn't see him being that idiotic either, yet sometimes even the best-trained soldiers did stupid things, and no matter how well trained by Leather the Doc was, he could still mess up.

That was why, when he plunged his knife into the man's stomach, he was certain it wasn't Acton, the silhouette of an AK-47 and his tall, gangly frame tipping him off.

He twisted the blade, eliciting a moan as Niner slapped a hand over the man's mouth, pushing him to the ground.

A gun cocked behind him.

"Don't move."

Niner slowly rose, raising his hands.

Shit.

Acton emerged from the shadows and grabbed the weapon pointed at the silhouette, having decided it had to be a friendly. He shoved it up and out of the way as he plunged his knife deep into the man's stomach several times, rapidly pushing and pulling it as he inflicted as much damage as he could, as quickly as he could, there no way to slit the man's throat from behind as he struggled for the weapon.

It was over as soon as it began, the man dropping to the ground with a groan, relinquishing his hold on the gun as he instead gripped his dripping innards.

Acton felt his mouth fill with bile as his stomach churned.

A flashlight shone on the body at his feet but he avoided looking at his handiwork. He had killed before, though not like this.

It was disturbing.

"You okay, Doc? You look a little green."

He swallowed, relief washing over him as he recognized the voice.

Niner!

He smiled. "Fancy meeting you here." He handed Niner the gun then flicked his own flashlight on. He pointed at the body. "Looks like I saved your life again."

Niner stared at him. "Huh?"

"Hanoi. That's at least two times now, if I'm not mistaken."

Niner grunted. "I think I've saved your ass more than that, but who's counting?"

Acton followed Niner back the way the operator had come. "Not the same. It's your job to save mine, not the other way around."

Atlas emerged from around a corner with Dawson, Acton feeling safe for the first time in what seemed forever. Handshakes were exchanged.

"Good to see you, Doc," rumbled the big man.

"You too. Did you hear? I saved Niner's life again."

Atlas laughed, Acton swearing the timbers shook from the vibration. "Of course you did. The little girly man needs all the help he can get."

Niner feigned a snap kick to the chestnuts. "Hey, I'll have you know I was only moments away from saving myself."

"Sure you were."

Acton smiled. "I guess we'll never know."

Another man, one that Acton recognized as a member of Laura's security team, joined them. "Message from Control. Professor Acton's still—" He paused. "Oh, hi, Professor, I see they found you."

"Yes, good to see you, Reese." Acton stared past him, not sure what he expected to find. "My wife? I assume you have her?"

Dawson shook his head. "She wasn't with the others."

Reese cleared his throat. "Sorry, Professor. Control said one hostile escaped a few minutes ago. He had Professor Palmer with him."

All the hope and optimism Acton had been filled with drained as he bent over, hands on his knees.

They still had her.

And now they had no reason to keep her alive.

He sucked in a deep breath and straightened. He looked at Dawson. "What the hell are we waiting for?"

Dawson smiled slightly. "Nothing I can think of."

Acton marched past them. "Good, then let's go get her!"

Belfast, South Africa

Tladi cursed as they approached his hometown, killing their speed as to not attract attention. It was a sleepy place, there not much to do, and that meant too many idle eyes. He had no clue what had happened in the mine. There had been a gunshot, a cry from one of his men, then the stranger walking past them, his hand over his flashlight.

Nothing else.

But the fact his eyes, glued on the rearview mirror the entire way, had spotted no sign of his men, suggested something horrible had happened.

And the bitch in the passenger seat was responsible.

Because of her and her friends, his brother was dead. It was true they didn't get along all the time, in fact, they rarely saw each other, it weeks, sometimes months between visits. He was to blame for that, never welcoming to him, Sipho a constant reminder of how he had failed in life, and what was possible with the upbringing provided by their mother.

He was a success.

Not rich by any means, but he had a good job, good pay, a humble though far nicer home than his troubled brother, and respect. On the rare occasions the two of them would go out together, people would come up to them and shake his brother's hand, thanking him for some good deed he had done for them in the past, or simply saying hello.

No one ever approached him.

No one ever thanked him.

The only reason he had a wife was because he had got her pregnant and the two mothers had got together to deal with the problem. His wife hated him, in fact, she feared him, but she was the poorest of the poor with nowhere to run. This wasn't the big city where you could just move to the other side and never see each other. This was Belfast, a tiny hole of a town where everybody knew everybody, where everybody knew everyone's business.

He could sense the eyes on him, judging him. Word had probably already spread of his brother's death, and now everyone would blame him despite there no possibility of anyone knowing he was involved.

His chest tightened as he realized that was no longer true. If someone had arrived at the mine, and his men had talked, they'd be coming for him.

They wouldn't talk. They know I'd kill them.

Yet they might. There was no loyalty out of kinship, only loyalty out of fear, a weak foundation if you feared someone else even more.

Prison in South Africa was a terrifying prospect, and his men definitely faced that if caught.

Poachers were scum.

He was scum.

I wish I were more like my brother.

He glanced at the white woman who had wisely kept her mouth shut the entire trip. It was a good thing. They hadn't found any evidence of the gold, and she was now worthless to him. He'd as soon kill her now, but he had a price to exact from her, and he intended to collect. She had treated him like dirt, showing no respect, and talking to him like he was an idiot.

And he was no idiot.

But an idiot would go home, like he was doing now.

He turned, there no point heading directly into the hands of the authorities who, if they weren't already waiting for him, would be arriving shortly. He could shoot it out, go down in a blaze of glory, but right now he needed time to think, to figure a way out of this.

If only Florence had known about the mine.

Then Jacob would have remembered where it was, they would have gone, they would have either found the gold or not, then moved on with their lives. His brother would be alive, his men would be free, and he'd still have time to meet his buyer next week and unload the months of work accumulated in his shed.

But she hadn't known.

And because of it, everything had gone to shit.

It would have been easier on her, too.

He glanced at the woman. "Do you think the gold was there?"

She shook her head. "No."

She sounded too certain for his liking. "Why?"

"Because the story made no sense. The Kruger Gold is supposed to be worth as much as half a billion dollars. That's an incredible amount. There's no way it was buried on a single farm, then moved by a lone farmer to a mine, like Marius Erasmus' grandmother described. The Kruger Gold either never existed, was moved to Europe and melted down like most think, or is still out there, somewhere."

"Then what were you looking for?"

She shrugged. "A clue. We found some coins. Those coins proved that *some* Kruger minted coins did exist at the time. Most likely what was originally buried on that farm was part of the greater shipment. You can't just move that much gold in a single go. You have to do it over time, in small batches. I think this was one of those."

His head bobbed slowly as he drove through the streets he had grown up on, realizing his dreams of untold riches were disappearing with each word from the woman's mouth. "So my brother died for nothing."

She stared at him. "Your brother died because of a few gold coins that might mean nothing, or might be a clue that leads to part of a long lost treasure. Either way he shouldn't have died."

Tladi ignored her implied criticism. If she and her friends hadn't been snooping around for gold, none of this would have happened.

It wasn't his fault.

And he wasn't going to die for it.

He just needed some place to think.

A thought dawned on him and he smiled.

Perfect!

En route to Belfast, South Africa

Dawson was content to let Niner drive, Jimmy, Leather, and Reese, escorting the rescued hostages to a rendezvous with consulate personnel and the South African authorities. It had been hard to get the Tasker girl off Acton, she clearly having taken to him in their time together, it sweet how she begged him to keep in touch, as if he were her only friend in the world.

The idea had him dwelling on Maggie once again, and what he'd do if he lost her. He remembered how in Paris he had lost the will to live, not caring if the rioters killed him, tore him apart—he just wanted it all to end so he could be with her once again.

But this time there would be no rampaging hordes of religious fanatics, no ancient cults or forgotten Nazis to take him to the next world.

There would only be him.

And suicide was something that would never be part of the equation. He loved life too much, loved his job too much, loved the guys in the Unit too much. If he were to lose Maggie, it would be the most devastating thing he had ever faced, but he'd face it, work through it, and honor her memory by moving on, continuing to do what he did every day, making the world a better place.

Though it was the job that concerned him. He knew he could become overwhelmed with emotion from what had happened in Paris. He had put his life at risk, and those of the others, by doing what he had. It was wrong, it a nearly fatal, selfish mistake, and it could never happen again.

He'd have to take himself out of the rotation, at least until he could trust himself to not be distracted.

Like now.

They were heading after the ringleader, Tladi, who still had Professor Palmer as a hostage.

Yet he wasn't planning on what to do, he was obsessing over Maggie.

And that was wrong.

There were too many other people's lives at stake to be distracted.

He was a soldier.

But he was also a man.

A lover.

And not knowing what was going to happen, was killing him.

He had to know.

He activated his comm. "Control, Zero-One, come in, over."

"Zero-One, Control, go ahead."

"Control, we're less than ten minutes from Belfast. Can I get an update on Maggie Harris?"

"No change in her condition, Zero-One."

"Copy that. Zero-One, out." Dawson frowned, leaning back in his seat and closing his eyes.

"What's wrong with Maggie?"

Dawson opened his eyes, turning his head slightly toward Acton. "They think a massive stroke." His chest hurt, it the first time he had said it aloud.

"Oh my God! Is she okay?"

He shook his head slightly. "We don't know yet." He looked away, watching the landscape whipping by, realizing that he was definitely going to have to remove himself from the roster if this was the way it was going to be.

He felt a hand on his shoulder. "Listen, if there's anything we can do, you let us know. And I mean *anything.*"

Dawson was torn. The professors were rich. Incredibly rich. They'd be able to provide access to the best of the best, whether that was doctors or facilities, and they'd be willing to do it, no questions asked. They had stepped up in the past without hesitation when his men were in need, and he knew they would do it again.

Yet this was different.

This was asking for a personal favor, for money from civilians. It went against everything he believed in. Before, when he had asked for help, or it had been offered, it was for the good of the mission, for the good of his men. Never had it been for a loved one, for anything personal.

But it's Maggie!

They could help her. They could save her. Whoever said money can't buy happiness might very well have been right—hell, he got paid a ridiculously meager salary for saving his country, yet he was happy. Because of Maggie.

But money *did* buy the best medical care.

Acton pulled his shoulder back slightly, forcing Dawson to turn his head toward the man. "I'll make this easy for you because I know you're not the type to ask. We're not helping you, we're helping *our* friend, Maggie, a civilian. Have them contact my friend Greg. You've met him. He'll arrange everything until we're back to take care of it ourselves."

Dawson stared into the man's eyes, a man he had once tried to kill, a man who had killed members of his team while defending himself, realizing at that very moment that this man truly was a friend, and that they would do anything for each other, as he would for any of his men.

Acton was part of the team.

He was part of the family.

And all he could say were two words, not trusting himself to say any more.

"Thank you."

Florence Mokoena Residence
Belfast, South Africa

Reading followed Ndlovu inside, the trembling woman who had answered the door clearly having received a fresh beating. It enraged him. If there was one thing in his entire time as a police officer that had affected him more than all the murders and gang violence, it was domestic abuse. Defenseless women beaten senseless by their husbands, too terrified to press charges because they knew the justice system would simply release their abuser in short order, to perhaps deliver a fatal beating as payment.

The worst was when he'd have to arrest one of these poor women for murdering her abuser, an act of self-preservation nonetheless illegal.

That was why, quite often, a story would be arrived at before a statement was taken.

It wasn't something he was proud of, but he'd be damned if a woman, beaten within inches of her life on multiple occasions, would go to prison for killing a man who one day soon would have done the same to her.

And right now, he wanted to take whoever had done this to the woman who stood in front of him, and bury him alive.

After he let her loose on him for a while.

"What's your name, dear?"

"F-Florence."

"Who did this to you?"

She turned her face away, trying to hide the evidence. "I-I don't know."

Reading pulled out a rickety chair, guiding her into it. He knelt in front of her, gently examining her wounds, there nothing life threatening or that might cause permanent damage, at least as far as he could tell, though whether there were internal injuries, he couldn't say. He glanced up at Ndlovu. "She needs to see a doctor."

Ndlovu nodded. "I'll arrange for one."

Reading looked at her. "Miss, was it someone you know?"

Again nothing.

"Miss, we can help you. Was it Tladi Tsabalala?"

She flinched, the name obviously meaning something to her, a name that elicited fear.

Reading knelt even lower, his knees killing him, his back violently protesting his efforts as he coaxed the information out of the woman with as gentle a voice as he could muster. "It was, wasn't it? What did he want to know?"

She fingered a medallion around her neck, it appearing new, the luster suggesting a recent acquisition, yet the way she gently caressed it implied a deeper connection than something so new should merit.

Maybe there was something else there before, that this replaced.

He nodded toward the medallion. "Did he want to know about that?"

She finally looked him in the eye. "About one like it."

"Why?"

She flipped it over, revealing the reversed imprint of something, something that meant little to him. "It-it secret to finding gold."

This caught Ndlovu's attention. "You mean the Kruger Gold?"

She nodded, warily eyeing the younger man.

Reading continued, she finally opening up. "What did you tell him?"

"O-only that my father found a coin, and that white people were excited. They go to farm to dig."

"What farm?"

"Farm my father work at."

Tires skidded on dirt outside, forcing Reading painfully to stand. "Are you expecting someone?"

She rapidly shook her head, her eyes wide with fear. "N-no!"

Ndlovu was already at the window, peering through a sliver in the curtains. "Two people. One male, local, one female, white. Looks like your Professor Palmer."

Reading looked about for a weapon, spotting a heavy cast iron frying pan sitting on a woodstove. He grabbed it, taking up position on the other side of the door as Ndlovu drew his weapon, stepping into the far corner to get a better angle on the new arrivals. Reading put his finger to his lips for the young woman's benefit. She nodded, terrified, as she sat frozen at her kitchen table.

The door swung open.

"Ahh, there you are."

Tladi stepped inside, Laura in front of him, blocking Ndlovu's shot. Tladi spotted him, reaching for a weapon tucked into his belt. Reading swung the pan, hard, smacking the man's head with a deafening thud. Tladi collapsed to the floor as Laura yelped, rushing deeper into the tiny, humble home the moment her captor's grip loosened on her.

Then she stopped, spinning around. "Hugh!" She rushed into his arms as Ndlovu kicked Tladi's weapon out of reach, it unnecessary, the poacher out cold. "Thank God you're here!"

Ndlovu slapped cuffs on Tladi, though not before Laura took a moment to hoof him in the stomach. She returned to Reading, giving him the biggest hug he could ever recall receiving. She pushed back, looking up at him. "Where's James?"

Reading's eyes narrowed. "Isn't he with you?"

Belfast, South Africa

Dawson was all business now, any thoughts of Maggie buried deep, there a job to do. Atlas and Acton headed for the back of the location, a shanty, for lack of a better word, on the edge of Belfast. The drone had tracked the poacher holding Laura Palmer to this location, his vehicle parked on an angle out front, the engine still hot.

He was here.

The UAV's infrared suggested there were five inside, all in a single room. A hostage appeared to be against the far wall, the hostiles sitting around a table in the center of the front room, whoever Tladi had met here clearly friends, perhaps the owner of the rental parked on the street.

He activated his comm. "Okay, quick and clean. Try not to kill the professor."

"Copy that," replied Atlas, now out of sight with Acton.

"Execute in three… two… one… execute!"

Niner booted the front door off its hinges and Dawson surged inside to sounds of Atlas and Acton entering from the rear. He aimed his scavenged weapon at the table, then smiled.

"Hold your fire!"

Atlas and Acton rushed into the room, both raising their weapons to the ceiling as Interpol Agent Hugh Reading held up a cup.

"Tea?"

Dawson laughed, Laura leaping from her seat, diving into her husband's arms, their reunion silent yet heartwarming.

And time-consuming.

He had to get home to Maggie.

Now.

He pointed at the man handcuffed against the wall. "I assume that's him?"

Laura broke away from Acton's embrace, nodding. "Yes, he's the one behind it all."

Reading gestured to the other man at the table. "This is Agent Ndlovu of the State Security Agency."

Dawson nodded. "Good. I assume you're going to handle things on this end?"

"You've rescued all the hostages?"

"Yes. The Americans are rendezvousing with consulate personnel, and the South Africans will be handed over to your people."

Ndlovu bowed slightly. "Then yes, I've got this end covered."

"Good." Dawson waved the others toward the door. "Let's go. I want to be stateside as soon as possible."

Somewhere over the Atlantic

Leather had wisely sent for Laura's private Gulfstream V to meet them in Johannesburg long before the rescue, the man not only a master at tactics, but logistics as well. He and his man were returning on a commercial flight to the dig site in Egypt, Leather having refused time off, despite taking one to the chest, the body armor leaving him with a nasty bruise, but little else.

Young Courtney Tasker had latched onto James, much to the amusement of Laura, when they all met at the consulate in Johannesburg, Courtney's father in Washington gratefully accepting Laura's offer of a much quicker flight home in her jet, rather than the back of a Herc, the Treasury Secretary also insisting Dawson and his men provide security for the flight.

That was clearly fine by him, getting him home sooner.

They were all exhausted and clearly concerned about Maggie, Laura noticing the usual joking around between the warriors subdued this time. Everyone had been running on adrenaline for so long, they were all crashing, heads drooping, eyes barely open.

Dawson bolted upright, pressing his finger against his ear.

"Go ahead, Control."

Everyone was instantly alert, Laura leaning forward in her seat.

"Okay, thank you. Zero-One, out."

He sat back in his seat, saying nothing. Niner broke the silence.

"Well?"

Dawson let out a long, slow breath, the toughest man Laura had ever met, struggling to maintain control. "She's going to survive."

His voice cracked as Laura's hand flew to her mouth, momentarily relieved, though sensing there was something more.

The others sensed it too.

Niner sat on the edge of the seat across from Dawson, lowering his voice. "But?"

"They don't know the extent of the brain damage. She's in a medically induced coma until they can figure out what went wrong."

The tears Dawson couldn't let out instead flowed down Laura's cheeks, her chest hurting as James squeezed her hand tightly. She looked over at the man she loved and pictured how she would feel if it were him lying in a sterile hospital room, hooked up to monitors, with a future of uncertainty ahead of them.

It was crushing.

She rose, walking down the aisle then kneeling in front of Dawson, taking his hand in hers and pressing it to her chin. She stared him in the eyes. "Whatever she needs, she gets."

A single tear rolled down Dawson's cheek, it quickly wiped away.

Womack Army Medical Center
Fort Bragg, North Carolina

The reunion between Courtney and her father had been a tearful one, and Acton had sensed a change in the girl. She had come over and given him a hug then a heartfelt apology to Laura for the way she had behaved. Laura had hugged the young woman, giving her a kiss on the top of the head, graciously accepting the apology, Courtney appearing genuinely relieved, and genuinely appreciative of the affection shown, Acton getting the sense it was lacking in her home life.

The pampered life of privilege, where nannies raise the children.

The heart-wrenching delivery of her boyfriend's body to his grieving parents had been something he could have lived without, though he had felt it his duty to witness it, as had the others. Experiencing their grief almost made him thankful he could never go through the loss of a child, though he recognized some of himself in them as he recalled the pain he had suffered when his beloved students had been killed in Peru by the very men who had just saved them.

He glanced at Dawson and his team, everyone in the waiting room of the hospital. Wives, children, and girlfriends were there, it truly a family, something only those who served, those who were the family of those who served, could understand. The military was a way of life, career military a calling, a lifetime of sacrifice for little thanks, thanks that wasn't desired or necessary, the reward the job and the knowledge that when they came home, they had done good, they had made the world a better place for the loved ones that waited behind that door.

And now, one of their own lay struggling for her life on the other side of the cold white walls of progress, the most highly skilled warriors in the world powerless in this battle, unable to do anything beyond provide the support only family could.

On their way to find Laura, Dawson had contacted his people, allowing Acton to place a call to Greg Milton who had taken care of everything, a specialist from New York here within hours, though they had yet to hear anything.

Instead, everyone kept each other distracted, small talk and cellphones filling the void.

Niner walked over to them. "So, Doc, you going back for the gold?"

Acton shook his head. "I think I've had my fill for now. Professor Ncube will lead a team to search the mines in the area. You never know, he might find it."

"How much are we talking about?"

"If you believe the conspiracy theories, half a billion."

Niner's eyes flew open. "Holy shit!" He turned to the others. "So, umm, I've got some leave coming up. Anyone want to go on safari?"

A dozen hands shot up in the air.

Niner turned to Acton. "So, if we found it, do we get to keep it?"

Acton chuckled. "You'll have to ask the South African government that one. If it's in the mine, then it's on government land, so probably not."

"Shit, then what's the point?"

Acton smiled. "The thrill of discovery? Of solving a mystery over a century old?"

Niner batted the words with his hand. "Bah, I'm more interested in solving my credit card problem."

Jimmy joined them. "Dude, with half a billion, you could solve all our credit card problems."

Niner tossed a thumb over his shoulder at Atlas. "We *might* have enough. You know him and comic books."

The others began to laugh when the door to the ICU opened, the specialist stepping out.

The room fell silent.

"Mr. Dawson?"

Dawson rose, everyone else not already standing, following suit. "Is she okay?"

His voice was one of desperation, something Acton had never heard from the man.

The doctor smiled. "She's going to be fine." He held up a finger as the room was about to erupt into cheers. "Eventually. She's got a long road to recovery ahead of her, but I'm confident in the end she'll be one hundred percent."

Dawson dropped into his chair, burying his head between his knees as he folded his hands behind his neck, everyone crowding around to pat him on the back, words of relief and encouragement exchanged. He rose, extending his hand. "Thanks, Doc, thanks for saving her."

The doctor shook his hand. "Don't thank me, thank those who found her. They got to her just in time. Your fiancée is one tough cookie, but she wouldn't have lasted much longer before there would have been permanent damage."

Dawson grabbed Red, giving him a bear hug, lifting the man off the floor before lowering him and pulling Spock and Sweets into the embrace, saying nothing. Acton took Laura's hand and squeezed as they silently witnessed a perfect moment.

Dawson let go, turning to the doctor. "This recovery, what's it involve?"

"A lot of physical therapy and retraining her brain. All her mental faculties are there, she just needs to relearn how to work her body. But don't worry, thanks to your friends, she'll get the best care possible."

Dawson turned to them, about to say something, his chin trembling, when Laura wisely saved him.

"No need to thank us. Anyone in our position would do the same." She looked at the doctor. "Can he see her?"

"Absolutely!"

Dawson bolted through the doors, leaving everyone in the waiting area to share their relief with each other.

Acton held Laura tight, gazing into her eyes. "I don't know what I'd do if I ever lost you."

She gazed up at him, smiling. "Then don't ever lose me."

He smiled. "Sounds like a plan to me."

Greater Kruger National Park, South Africa

Gatsha pushed through the thick brush, finding the opening exactly as he had suspected. A few moments earlier he had spotted several bats fly out from behind the bushes, something having startled them.

And bats didn't rest in bushes.

"What is it?" asked his younger brother.

"Not sure. Looks like a cave or something." Gatsha stepped inside, letting his eyes adjust for a moment. Something stared out of the darkness at him, sending him jumping backward with a yelp.

"What is it?" asked his brother, pushing past him, eager to discover what could scare his older brother, the boy too stupid to know fear should be respected.

He screamed, it blood curdling.

Gatsha hauled him back a few paces.

"Is-is he dead?"

Gatsha smacked his brother's shoulder with the back of his hand. "Stupid question. Of course he's dead. He's nothing but bones." Gatsha knelt beside the skeleton, little left of the clothes the man had once worn.

"I wonder how long he's been here."

Gatsha shrugged. "Dunno. Long time, I think."

"What's this?" His brother reached forward and pulled a rolled up piece of paper from the man's hand. "I think there's writing on it."

"What's it say?"

His brother shrugged. "I don't know, you're the one who can read."

Gatsha took the paper and stepped back outside and into the light. He unrolled it, the dried paper splitting in two.

"Careful!"

"Well, stop crowding me!"

"What does it say?"

Gatsha shoved his brother away, holding up the paper, his eyes widening.

"My dearest Dania,

"It is said the wages of sin is death, but the gift of God is eternal life through Jesus Christ our Lord."

"What does that mean?"

Gatsha shrugged. "I don't know. If you'd shut up, I could finish."

His brother pouted. "You don't have to be so mean."

Gatsha felt bad. "Sorry. Can I finish?"

His brother brightened. "Yes!"

"I both fear and hope these words are true, as so many have died tonight to preserve our nation's future that I fear the price paid has been too high, though I make this sacrifice willingly. My only regret is that I will never again see your beautiful smile when I wake in the morning, or hear the joy of my little girls as they greet the new day.

"I am a God-fearing man, as you know, and I trust that my sacrifice in his name will guarantee our reunion in Heaven, where I can once again hold you in my arms, smell your sweet sweet hair, and hear the laughter of our children as they play.

"Be strong, and forgive me for leaving you alone.

"Love Boet"

"Gatsha, time to eat!"

Gatsha glanced over his shoulder, his mother waving at them. He tossed the letter back in the cave then grabbed his brother, his stomach rumbling at the prospect of the promised picnic.

THE END

ACKNOWLEDGEMENTS

I really enjoyed writing this one. I was, of course, familiar with Krugerrands from my Lethal Weapon love affair (and check out Get the Gringo—awesome!), but less so with the legend of the Kruger Gold. That this treasure existed, is of little doubt. A nation's gold doesn't just disappear. The question is what happened to it. Some claim it made it to Europe, others claim only some did, and many claim none. No matter what happened to the gold, it is clear that it is a mystery yet to be solved.

Though perhaps it has.

A recent article claims it might have been found. You can read more about that here:

http://www.telegraph.co.uk/news/worldnews/1311874/Town-under-siege-as-missing-Kruger-gold-is-found-on-farm.html

Here's a fun anecdote related to this story. At one point Niner refers to Dawson as the "ultimate male". These words weren't randomly chosen. Years ago, I bought my wife a cellphone—long before smartphones were a reality. I programmed in my cellphone number, and as a joke, set the name to "THE ULTIMATE MALE". She thought this was hilarious, and of course assured me it was completely true, and I believe her to this day.

But the comedy comes later, a few years later, when my rapier wit has been forgotten.

I bought my wife a new phone.

And gave the old one to our daughter.

Who wondered why she was getting calls from THE ULTIMATE MALE, and her dad would be on the other end of the line when she answered it.

Fortunately, she was too young to have to explain it to her, and I reprogrammed the phone.

And one other fun anecdote. When Jeb the janitor is thinking about high school locker rooms, and how bad the girls were, that comes from the real-life experiences of a friend who, when times were tough, became a janitor after losing everything due to 9/11. I won't give his name to protect his privacy, but he knows who he is.

There are a *lot* of people to thank on this one. My dad of course for much of the research, Bob Crampton, the inventor of the Damfino, Angela Lee for her suggestion of a place Hugh Reading might order take-out from, and what he might order, Peter Harman for pairing food with drink, Lindy Jones Zywot for some Briticisms, Greg "Chief" Michael for treasure hunting advice, Brent Richards for hand-to-hand combat advice and an ammo primer, Deborah Wilson for equine advice, and last but definitely not least, Marc Quesnel and his lovely wife Mitzi, along with her Zulu colleagues, who were instrumental in the South African research that went into this book. Many thanks to them, and any errors are mine and mine alone.

To those who have not already done so, please visit my website at www.jrobertkennedy.com then sign up for the Insider's Club to be notified of new book releases. Your email address will never be shared or sold and you'll only receive the occasional email from me as I don't have time to spam you!

Thank you once again for reading.

ABOUT THE AUTHOR

With over 500,000 books in circulation and over 3000 five-star reviews, USA Today bestselling author J. Robert Kennedy has been ranked by Amazon as the #1 Bestselling Action Adventure novelist based upon combined sales. He is the author of over twenty-five international bestsellers including the smash hit James Acton Thrillers. He lives with his wife and daughter and writes full-time.

Visit Robert's website at www.jrobertkennedy.com for the latest news and contact information, and to join the Insider's Club to be notified when new books are released.

Available James Acton Thrillers

The Protocol (Book #1)

For two thousand years, the Triarii have protected us, influencing history from the crusades to the discovery of America. Descendent from the Roman Empire, they pervade every level of society, and are now in a race with our own government to retrieve an ancient artifact thought to have been lost forever.

Brass Monkey (Book #2)

A nuclear missile, lost during the Cold War, is now in play--the most public spy swap in history, with a gorgeous agent the center of international attention, triggers the end-game of a corrupt Soviet Colonel's twenty five year plan. Pursued across the globe by the Russian authorities, including a brutal Spetsnaz unit, those involved will stop at nothing to deliver their weapon, and ensure their payday, regardless of the terrifying consequences.

Broken Dove (Book #3)

With the Triarii in control of the Roman Catholic Church, an organization founded by Saint Peter himself takes action, murdering one of the new Pope's operatives. Detective Chaney, called in by the Pope to investigate, disappears, and, to the horror of the Papal staff sent to inform His Holiness, they find him missing too, the only clue a secret chest, presented to each new pope on the eve of their election, since the beginning of the Church.

The Templar's Relic (Book #4)

The Vault must be sealed, but a construction accident leads to a miraculous discovery--an ancient tomb containing four Templar Knights, long forgotten, on the grounds of the Vatican. Not knowing who they can trust, the Vatican requests Professors James Acton and Laura Palmer examine the find, but what they discover, a precious Islamic relic, lost during the Crusades, triggers a set of events that shake the entire world, pitting the two greatest religions against each other. At risk is nothing less than the Vatican itself, and the rock upon which it was built.

Flags of Sin (Book #5)

Archaeology Professor James Acton simply wants to get away from everything, and relax. A trip to China seems just the answer, and he and his fiancée, Professor Laura Palmer, are soon on a flight to Beijing. But while boarding, they bump into an old friend, Delta Force Command Sergeant Major Burt Dawson, who surreptitiously delivers a message that they must meet the next day, for Dawson knows something they don't. China is about to erupt into chaos.

The Arab Fall (Book #6)

An accidental find by a friend of Professor James Acton may lead to the greatest archaeological discovery since the tomb of King Tutankhamen, perhaps even greater. And when news of it spreads, it reaches the ears of a group hell-bent on the destruction of all idols and icons, their mere existence considered blasphemous to Islam.

The Circle of Eight (Book #7)

The Bravo Team is targeted by a madman after one of their own intervenes in a rape. Little do they know this internationally well-respected banker is also a senior member of an organization long thought extinct, whose stated goals for a reshaped world are not only terrifying, but with today's globalization, totally achievable.

The Venice Code (Book #8)

A former President's son is kidnapped in a brazen attack on the streets of Potomac by the very ancient organization that murdered his father, convinced he knows the location of an item stolen from them by the late president. A close friend awakes from a coma with a message for archaeology Professor James Acton from the same organization, sending him on a quest to find an object only rumored to exist, while trying desperately to keep one step ahead of a foe hell-bent on possessing it.

Pompeii's Ghosts (Book #9)

Two thousand years ago Roman Emperor Vespasian tries to preserve an empire by hiding a massive treasure in the quiet town of Pompeii should someone challenge his throne. Unbeknownst to him nature is about to unleash its wrath upon the Empire during which the best and worst of Rome's citizens will be revealed during a time when duty and honor were more than words, they were ideals worth dying for.

Amazon Burning (Book #10)

Days from any form of modern civilization, archaeology Professor James Acton awakes to gunshots. Finding his wife missing, taken by a member of one of the uncontacted tribes, he and his friend INTERPOL Special Agent Hugh Reading try desperately to find her in the dark of the jungle, but quickly realize there is no hope without help. And with help three days away, he knows the longer they wait, the farther away she'll be.

The Riddle (Book #11)

Russia accuses the United States of assassinating their Prime Minister in Hanoi, naming Delta Force member Sergeant Carl "Niner" Sung as the assassin. Professors James Acton and Laura Palmer, witnesses to the murder, know the truth, and as the Russians and Vietnamese attempt to use the situation to their advantage on the international stage, the husband and wife duo attempt to find proof that their friend is innocent.

Blood Relics (Book #12)

A DYING MAN. A DESPERATE SON.
ONLY A MIRACLE CAN SAVE THEM BOTH.

Professor Laura Palmer is shot and kidnapped in front of her husband, archaeology Professor James Acton, as they try to prevent the theft of the world's Blood Relics, ancient artifacts thought to contain the blood of Christ, a madman determined to possess them all at any cost.

Sins of the Titanic (Book #13)

THE ASSEMBLY IS ETERNAL. AND THEY'LL STOP AT NOTHING TO KEEP IT THAT WAY.

When Professor James Acton is contacted about a painting thought to have been lost with the sinking of the Titanic, he is inadvertently drawn into a century old conspiracy an ancient organization known as The Assembly will stop at nothing to keep secret.

Saint Peter's Soldiers (Book #14)

A MISSING DA VINCI.
A TERRIFYING GENETIC BREAKTHROUGH.
A PAST AND FUTURE ABOUT TO COLLIDE!

In World War Two a fabled da Vinci drawing is hidden from the Nazis, those involved fearing Hitler may attempt to steal it for its purported magical powers. It isn't returned for over fifty years.

And today, archaeology Professor James Acton and his wife are about to be dragged into the terrible truth of what happened so many years ago, for the truth is never what it seems, and the history we thought was fact, is all lies.

The Thirteenth Legion (Book #15)

A TWO-THOUSAND-YEAR-OLD DESTINY IS ABOUT TO BE FULFILLED!

USA Today bestselling author J. Robert Kennedy delivers another action-packed thriller in The Thirteenth Legion. After Interpol Agent Hugh Reading spots his missing partner in Berlin, it sets off a chain of events that could lead to the death of his best friends, and if the legends are true, life as we know it.

Raging Sun (Book #16)

WILL A SEVENTY-YEAR-OLD MATTER OF HONOR TRIGGER THE NEXT GREAT WAR?

The Imperial Regalia have been missing since the end of World War Two, and the Japanese government, along with the new—and secretly illegitimate—emperor, have been lying to the people. But the truth isn't out yet, and the Japanese will stop at nothing to secure their secret and retrieve the ancient relics confiscated by a belligerent Russian government. Including war.

Wages of Sin (Book #17)

WHEN IS THE PRICE TO PROTECT A NATION'S LEGACY TOO HIGH?

Jim and Laura are on safari in South Africa when a chance encounter leads to a clue that could unlock the greatest mystery remaining of the Boer War over a century ago—the location to over half a billion dollars in gold!

Available Special Agent Dylan Kane Thrillers

Rogue Operator (Book #1)

Three top secret research scientists are presumed dead in a boating accident, but the kidnapping of their families the same day raises questions the FBI and local police can't answer, leaving them waiting for a ransom demand that will never come. Central Intelligence Agency Analyst Chris Leroux stumbles upon the story, finding a phone conversation that was never supposed to happen, and is told to leave it to the FBI. But he can't let it go. For he knows something the FBI doesn't. One of the scientists is alive.

Containment Failure (Book #2)

New Orleans has been quarantined, an unknown virus sweeping the city, killing one hundred percent of those infected. The Centers for Disease Control, desperate to find a cure, is approached by BioDyne Pharma who reveal a former employee has turned a cutting edge medical treatment capable of targeting specific genetic sequences into a weapon, and released it. The stakes have never been higher as Kane battles to save not only his friends and the country he loves, but all of mankind.

Cold Warriors (Book #3)

While in Chechnya CIA Special Agent Dylan Kane stumbles upon a meeting between a known Chechen drug lord and a retired General once responsible for the entire Soviet nuclear arsenal. Money is exchanged for a data stick and the resulting transmission begins a race across the globe to discover just what was sold, the only clue a reference to a top-secret Soviet weapon called Crimson Rush.

Death to America (Book #4)

America is in crisis. Dozens of terrorist attacks have killed or injured thousands, and worse, every single attack appears to have been committed by an American citizen in the name of Islam.

A stolen experimental F-35 Lightning II is discovered by CIA Special Agent Dylan Kane in China, delivered by an American soldier reported dead years ago in exchange for a chilling promise.

And Chris Leroux is forced to watch as his girlfriend, Sherrie White, is tortured on camera, under orders to not interfere, her continued suffering providing intel too valuable to sacrifice.

Black Widow (Book #5)

USA Today bestselling author J. Robert Kennedy serves up another heart-pounding thriller in Black Widow. After corrupt Russian agents sell deadly radioactive Cesium to Chechen terrorists, CIA Special Agent Dylan Kane is sent to infiltrate the ISIL terror cell suspected of purchasing it. Then all contact is lost.

Available Delta Force Unleashed Thrillers

Payback (Book #1)

The daughter of the Vice President is kidnapped from an Ebola clinic, triggering an all-out effort to retrieve her by America's elite Delta Force just hours after a senior government official from Sierra Leone is assassinated in a horrific terrorist attack while visiting the United States. As she battles impossible odds and struggles to prove her worth to her captors who have promised she will die, she's forced to make unthinkable decisions to not only try to save her own life, but those dying from one of the most vicious diseases known to mankind, all in the hopes an unleashed Delta Force can save her before her captors enact their horrific plan on an unsuspecting United States.

Infidels (Book #2)

When the elite Delta Force's Bravo Team is inserted into Yemen to rescue a kidnapped Saudi prince, they find more than they bargained for—a crate containing the Black Stone, stolen from Mecca the day before. Requesting instructions on how to proceed, they find themselves cut off and disavowed, left to survive with nothing but each other to rely upon.

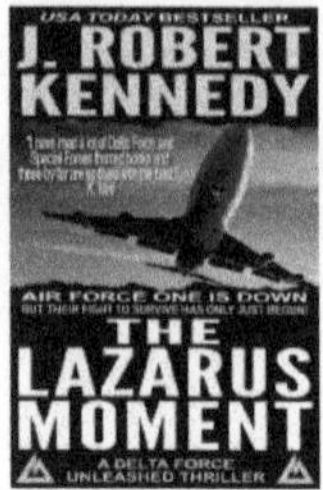

The Lazarus Moment (Book #3)

AIR FORCE ONE IS DOWN.
BUT THEIR FIGHT TO SURVIVE HAS ONLY JUST BEGUN!

When Air Force One crashes in the jungles of Africa, it is up to America's elite Delta Force to save the survivors not only from rebels hell-bent on capturing the President, but Mother Nature herself.

Kill Chain (Book #4)

WILL A DESPERATE PRESIDENT RISK WAR
TO SAVE HIS ONLY CHILD?

In South Korea, the President's daughter disappears aboard an automated bus carrying the spouses of the world's most powerful nations, hacked by an unknown enemy with an unknown agenda. In order to save all that remains of his family, the widower president unleashes America's elite Delta Force to save his daughter, yet the more they learn, the more the mystery deepens, witness upon witness declaring with certainty they never saw any kidnappers—only drones.

Available Detective Shakespeare Mysteries

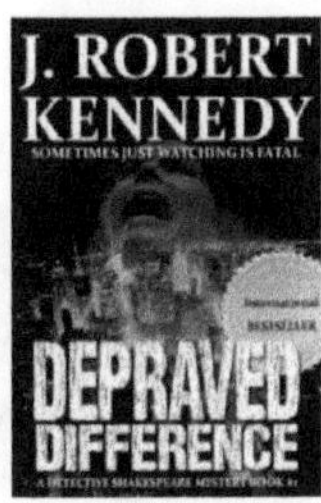

Depraved Difference (Book #1)

SOMETIMES JUST WATCHING IS FATAL

When a young woman is brutally assaulted by two men on the subway, her cries for help fall on the deaf ears of onlookers too terrified to get involved, her misery ended with the crushing stomp of a steel-toed boot. A cellphone video of her vicious murder, callously released on the Internet, its popularity a testament to today's depraved society, serves as a trigger, pulled a year later, for a killer.

Tick Tock (Book #2)

SOMETIMES HELL IS OTHER PEOPLE

Crime Scene tech Frank Brata digs deep and finds the courage to ask his colleague, Sarah, out for coffee after work. Their good time turns into a nightmare when Frank wakes up the next morning covered in blood, with no recollection of what happened, and Sarah's body floating in the tub.

The Redeemer (Book #3)

SOMETIMES LIFE GIVES MURDER A SECOND CHANCE

It was the case that destroyed Detective Justin Shakespeare's career, beginning a downward spiral of self-loathing and self-destruction lasting half a decade. And today things are only going to get worse. The Widow Rapist is free on a technicality, and it is up to Detective Shakespeare and his partner Amber Trace to find the evidence, five years cold, to put him back in prison before he strikes again.

Zander Varga, Vampire Detective

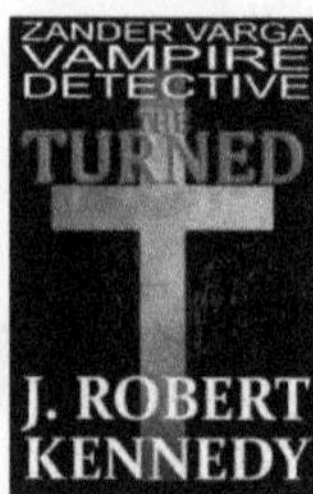

The Turned (Book #1)

Zander has relived his wife's death at the hands of vampires every day for almost three hundred years, his perfect memory a curse of becoming one of The Turned—infecting him their final heinous act after her murder. Nineteen year-old Sydney Winter knows Zander's secret, a secret preserved by the women in her family for four generations. But with her mother in a coma, she's thrust into the frontlines, ahead of her time, to fight side-by-side with Zander.

Printed in the USA
CPSIA information can be obtained
at www.ICGtesting.com
LVHW040902300824
789700LV00047B/193

9 781537 533193